MARIANA ROMO-CARMONA
SPEAKING LIKE AN IMMIGRANT
A COLLECTION

Latina Lesbian History Project
New York City

Juanita (Ramos) Díaz, Director
Elizabeth Crespo-Kebler, Project Editor
Taina Del Valle and Ana Hidalgo, Production and Distribution
Assistants

First Edition, First Printing.
Library of Congress Catalog Card Number: 9875487
Romo-Carmona, Mariana, b. 1952
Speaking like an Immigrant: A Collection
ISBN 0-9619450-3-6

Published in the U.S.A. by the Latina Lesbian History Project (LLHP), a project of Latina Women's Educational Resources, Binghampton, NY 13905. For book orders and inquiries, write to LLHP, P.O. Box 850, New York, NY 10002

Cover painting: Adriana M. Romo
Cover design and back cover photo by June Chan

Other titles published by LLHP: *Compañeras: Latina Lesbians (An Anthology)*, 1987, edited by Juanita Ramos
2nd Edition by Routledge, Chapman & Hall, 1994

Dedicatoria/Dedication

This book is dedicated to the compañera Aida Esther
Santiago(1957-1997), who died of cancer one month after her
40th birthday. She was a Black Puertorriqueña, teacher, activist,
martial artist, breast cancer survivor, and co-founder of the
Latina lesbian group, Las Buenas Amigas.

Acknowledgments/Agradecimientos

My deep gratitude to my parents for having the strength to be
immigrants. To June Chan for being the only one in the world
like herself. To Juanita (Ramos) Díaz for being the guiding
force behind LLHP, and Elizabeth Crespo-Kebler for her
vision as editor. To Pedro Pietri for writing "Puerto Rican
Obituary." To Gloria Anzaldúa for the inspiration of her
writing. To all the Latinas and Latinos who took me in when I
had no country. To Chile.

୨ଌ

Also by Mariana Romo-Carmona
Living at Night
a novel

Grateful acknowledgment is made to the editors of the publications in which the following stories originally appeared: "Fear" appeared as "Untitled" in *Fight Back! Feminist Resistance to Male Violence*, Cleis Press, 1981; "Gabriela"(original in Spanish), *Compañeras: Latina Lesbians*, Latina Lesbian History Project, 1987 and 2nd ed. Routledge,1994; English translation of "Gabriela" by the author, *Conditions: 15*, 1988; "La virgen en el desierto" (original in Spanish), *Cuentos: Stories by Latinas*, Kitchen Table Press, 1983, "The Virgin in the Desert" English translation by the author in *Beyond Gender and Geography: American Women Writers*, East West Press, New Delhi, 1994; "2280", *Conditions: 17*, 1990; "Orphans", *Queer City*, The Portable Lower East Side, 1992; "The Web", *COLORLife* magazine, 1994; "Speaking Like an Immigrant" appeared as "Meditations on Immigration," in *Front*, Vancouver Arts Magazine, 1996.

The National Astraea Foundation's Lesbian Writers Fund Award, 1991, made possible the first draft of this manuscript.
Many thanks to the musician, Alex Adrian, for the gift of his reminiscences, which inspired "Contraband."

SPEAKING LIKE AN IMMIGRANT
CONTENTS

Introduction

Speaking Like An Immigrant takes us through a journey that flows through geographic and cultural spaces that are ever present within each other, the Chile of the past and the new lands of the present. The Chile of the author is in New York as well as in the lands of witches or memories of adolescence she conjures, and they become part of one another. The speaking done in this book does not conform to the voice of the immigrant imagined in the conventional vision of the "American Dream." Mariana Romo-Carmona's voice evokes dreams that defy, unmask, and force us to rethink customary knowledge. The unmasking of conventions presented in this collection does not limit itself to revealing the racism, sexism and heterosexism of the most reactionary visions of that American Dream. Through these narratives, the author also questions assumptions of unitary, monolithic subjects and conventional forms of activism coming from feminist and lesbian paradigms.

Speaking like an Immigrant exposes the fallacies of the "American Dream" portrayed in the mass media as access to the latest sportswear advertised by the superstars, comfortable homes, and hi tech entertainment, the symbols of status, happiness and well being promised to those that follow the work ethic. In the title story, the narrator is admonished to "work hard," to avoid ending up shining shoes on the Staten Island ferry. The surreal narrator of "The Web," explains her alienation as a loss of connection: "We have all but stopped speaking the language of our mother . . . I can't live alone without the web." In her futuristic vision of the "northern continent" in "2280," Romo-Carmona demystifies the "glowing, polished land of opportunity;" her vision of the future does not mirror the promise of progress that space age technology offers. In her narratives, Romo-Carmona presents a reality experienced by more and more Americans in the United States who, in spite of working hard and long hours, find that the gap between their earnings and those of the rich continue to widen.

To be successful, immigrants are told, you must become American, you must assimilate; this is the key to the "American Dream" as presented by dominant cultural paradigms. This vision of becoming American means to leave behind, to rid oneself of the past and look forward to something better. This "dream" imposes a fragmentation of the self. Those parts of our personal and collective histories lived prior to coming to the United States are deemed worthless, inferior and many times even shameful. This "dream" makes us invisible and produces the feeling of never belonging, of being faceless, voiceless. Becoming an American is to become someone without a past, without a history. As Romo-Carmona says, "It doesn't matter what country I'm from, to you they're all the same."

The term American as used in the United States evokes images of dominance and hegemony. It attempts to make insignificant the other peoples and parts of the globe that are also

America. The "dream" that has been constructed of "America" has attempted to erase the history of the colonization of Native Americans and Mexicans who inhabited this territory prior to the existence of the United States of America; to blot out the fact that this country was built through an economy based on the enslavement of African people. It forgets the history of brutal exclusion of Chinese at the turn of the century when the slogan unfurled by political parties and labor unions was "the Chinese must go." The lynch mobs that hung Chinese immigrants on lamp posts and burned entire Chinese communities on the West coast are also not remembered. The "dream" obviates the internment of US citizens of Japanese origin in concentration camps. It has attempted to conceal the history of colonization of Puerto Rico, the Philippines and the ongoing exploitation of "third world labor."

The voice that we hear in *Speaking like an Immigrant* takes us back to Chile. It is a trip through the desert with Mamá, through narrow roads that lead to mountain villages where there are flowers and ice, rivers, ravines, and "rock walls so tall that streams of water broke from the stone." We hear stories of ancient times and the people of the sun. We visit churches where miracles occur, uncover tombs and learn of lost travelers who wander for eternity in the sand. We learn about life and death and the wonders of the world through the eyes of a child. Chile, Mamá, el abuelo y la abuela, Gabriela y Susana, are vital forces that are necessary to capture the present and alleviate the pain of feeling alien.

Mariana Romo-Carmona's stories and poems lead us outside the constraints of a space where we are asked to deny parts of ourselves and fragment our lives. She situates herself in the interstices of geographic and cultural boundaries to seek refuge

iii

from the splits and fissures imposed by world views that define us as foreigners, excluded, invisible, not American and therefore, people who do not belong. This new place is one inhabited by a multiplicity of realities and identities that constitute experiences of wholeness. In this book Mariana Romo-Carmona captures experiences that are not only hers but that of many immigrants whose lives are both here and there, and present in their journeys.

The memories of Chile captured in these stories are more than those of a physical and cultural space that is yearned for. In "The Virgin in the Desert," these memories are set against the backdrop of the corruption of local politicians and government officials and the discrimination against immigrants crossing the desert from Bolivia. The churches described still evoke the brutal history of Spanish colonization after almost five centuries. The more recent history of the jailing and tortures of the thousands who "disappeared" under the Pinochet regime is presented in "Dream of Something Lost."

Memories of Chile are also presented through lesbian voices. The awakening of erotic love described in "Gabriela" is inextricably tied to the countryside of Chile. The physical and cultural space Romo-Carmona describes is etched into the exhilaration of the young bodies aroused by the first touch of another woman. As Romo-Carmona writes, she appropriates the being that has been made invisible and voiceless by heterosexism. At the same time, the author poses questions that lead us away from conventional definitions that come from within the lesbian community itself. What is a lesbian of color? What is that experience that lesbians of color are expected to articulate, the ones everyone wants to hear in a language we can all understand? What constitutes lesbian of color activism? As the character in "Welcome to America" attempts to take a cab uptown in mid-day traffic to attend to her mother's medical emergency, her existential dilemmas revolve around issues that seem far removed from making posters and protesting for civil rights. Discovering, understanding and appropriating lesbian and immigrant as vital, diverse and intertwined experiences is a process that the reader comes to know throughout the pages of this book.

In *Speaking like an Immigrant* we discover realities of many dimensions, multifaceted characters, and a wide range of experiences that contrast with the homogenization that characterizes stereotypes of immigrants, of women and of lesbians. In Romo-Carmona's narrative, we experience fear, poverty and abandonment, but we also live hope, love, passion and unity with nature. We bridge realities that seem distant and find connections between people who seem to have very little in common.

Speaking like an Immigrant is both timely and urgent in the political climate in which we live where the words foreigner and immigrant have increasingly become racialized. The speaking done in this book challenges the growing racist and xenophobic forces that wish to instill fear and hatred towards immigrants. While yesterday's immigrants are constructed as white and European, many more that come to the United States today are brown and from countries of the Third World. Previous immigrants are portrayed as having successfully assimilated, while today's are seen as foreigners and aliens. Although they are a smaller proportion of the total United States population than they were at the beginning of the twentieth century, in talk shows and senate hearings we are presented with the image of hordes who will take over the country. Folks who do not wish to openly point to the color of the more recent immigrants, argue that their concerns about immigration are economic. Those people, the argument goes, place an undue burden on public services. It is convenient and easy to forget that immigrants satisfy a demand for labor and pay taxes. Those bold enough to unabashedly object to the color of today's immigrant population argue that an ethnic revolution is taking place. They claim that the growth of the Latino and Asian populations in the United States will alter the racial make up of this country making whites no longer a majority. They remind us that the founding fathers envisioned a white society, not a multiethnic one, and they wish to keep it that way.

In the national political discourse, then, immigrants have become non persons; they have no rights although they contribute their labor to this society. Border patrol vehicles chase people crossing on foot until they are tired and can no longer run. "Tonk," the repeated sound of heavy flashlights hitting the heads of would be crossers in the night, has become the derogatory slang for Latino immigrant. Private citizens on the United States side of the border stage protests against immigration by shining bright lights toward Mexico to expose those waiting to cross. They are answered with mirrors that reflect the lights back on the United States as if to bare the hypocrisy of anti-immigration policies. As the economic boundaries between the United States and Third World countries have been modified to facilitate the flows of capital and profits, the flow of people has also increased. While the first is hailed as a positive and civilizing mission that brings progress to the world, the people whose previous forms of subsistence have been eliminated are considered dispensable. The flow of capital must remain uninhibited, while the flow of people must be brutally restrained. The current wave of anti-immigrant hatred is directed toward people who fit the stereotype of immigrant whether they are citizens or not, whether they are immigrants or have lived in the United States for centuries.

The author's use of English, Spanish, and her translations represents a writer's voice always in transition; it reflects a consciousness hewn from both languages and captures the forces that give life to her writing. In this way as well, this book reaffirms a different dream. Many immigrants have lost the language of their parents because of pressures to assimilate or because they have succumbed to the association of Spanish with deficiency and remediation. Romo-Carmona defies stereotypical images and speaks like an immigrant, a person who has claimed her past and her present, her ability to be whole, an agent of change. For Mariana Romo-Carmona, writing is a vehicle to break dominant paradigms. The re-ordering she has achieved transcends her own experiences and traces paths towards new understandings of inclusion.

Elizabeth Crespo-Kebler
Puerto Rico and Central Pennsylvania, 1998

❧

vii

You must know I'm South American, though I live here. A lifetime denying I'm exotic, a lifetime to become one with my own eyes. Yet my character *is* dark, my moods swing wildly, and I expect nothing from life save the satisfaction of knowing I expected the worst. There, I've confirmed it, and now perhaps this will explain me to you, so that I won't have to define my impulses in mid-sentence.

Sentence, there is a word, heavy with meaning. I revel in meaning, the signification of things, what is meant by signs that we observe in life and understand without anyone having to tell us; we simply know. This knowledge had been away from me for a long time, or rather, *I* had been away, until recently. Until I went back to the place I was born and came back here, helpless, full of signs, symbols, and meaning.

I returned thinking I had killed the part of me that contained a soul; I wandered dangerously, I watched the rain wet the sidewalks without falling. That is, the streets were wet, the sky was gray, and the leaves were blown about by the wind carrying water in its wake. Rain water. People walked among wet ivy and

1

wrought iron gates, the fumes of buses, and the impending moisture in the air. I thought, how like the country of my birth. I ached to go inside. I had been looking for a place like this. Simple. Steeped in the meaning of memories, but I resisted. In the bushes, beyond the ivy, dark red berries shivered, weighted down by the rain, I could not withstand the feeling that pulled me away from myself.

When we first arrived, so many years ago, my father said, start now, start working now, because you don't want to end up like that old guy on the Staten Island ferry saying "shine," to all the passengers. I worked very hard, my father was right. I see the guy now, it's another guy but he says the same thing, "shine," even if you're wearing suede, sandals, he doesn't care. He says, "shine," that's his job.

So you have to understand. I've reduced my whole life to one moment; it's what I'm fated to do, being South American. A million jobs and a million questions, but it doesn't matter what country I'm from, to you they're all the same. Uruguay, I tell you, and you light up and say, oh yeah, my cousin, he has a dentist, and his wife is from Brasil!

So many jobs I had. I cleaned shit, I dug holes, I taught Math, and I drove a bus. And all is reduced to the moment when I walked in, shutting the rain outside, the wind whistling in behind me. I blended with the darkness that isn't dark, that is soft light coming from somewhere, caressing my face, luring me gently with the smells of the place. Smells that are old and not mine, but mine all the same, known to my skin, and the silence that is balm in my heart as the murmuring goes on. And on, it never stops. Yet it is quiet in here.

I worked very hard, for many years, to give my voice another sound, my body another shape, but here I am, my whole life in

2

this one moment when my body slides right through these doors, blends in the dark, fits like leather along these worn benches-- all except the kneeling. I won't kneel, but I will succumb to the sound, let it take my soul if it has to, and it comes like waves: Dios te salve María llena eres de gracia-- Santa María Madre de Dios (Holy Mary full of Grace-- Holy Mary Mother of God.)

It is not religion I'm after, understand. Who am I? One of the old men huddled in the back, the guy on the ferry even, offering shoeshines, or one of the old women dressed in brown, kneeling up front, chanting the same song forever.

But I did return and I have seen that other face that awaited me there. Asunción, I might say to you. San Carlos or Bariloche. Cuzco, Cochabamba, or Quintay, a little fishing village. And, oh, you will reply, I know! My brother-in-law, he was in the Peace Corps!

Now I've seen the other face and I know who I would have been. My moods swing wildly and the features of my character seem deeper, the more I look. I could be anyone, the old man, the old woman, Santa María Madre de Dios-- Shoeshine! The rain that falls without falling, the silence that calms without speaking. I never knew I searched for something so simple, that reflection from the window; slide on the bench but don't kneel. There's no need except, depth is silence, depth is water, water like glass, glass like a mirror. The more I look I become one with my eyes. This is what I see. My features. Glass. Mirror. Eyes.

The more I look.

The darker they become.

෧

Original in Spanish
"La virgen en el desierto"
Cuentos: Stories by Latinas

La señora had died saying hardly a word to anyone. We learned everything through her son. From time to time, she would try to speak to my mother, or perhaps she cried a little. It was very hard to hear above the noise of the truck. Later, I could hear almost too well, while I pretended to fall asleep in my room, waiting for the boy who hadn't slept in four nights to cry. He sat quietly in the kitchen with Mamá, who always knows what to say. Not me, I didn't even know what to think, whether to fall asleep or stay awake. I only wanted the thin boy to cry, the one who hadn't slept in four nights.

La señora wore her long hair gathered in a bun, and Mamá had her leaning against her arms so she could breathe better. I think sometimes la señora would whisper something. I would lean over and strain to hear it. We were all thinking, and that was the only thing we could hear above the rumble of the engine. I still feel the vibration of the vehicle traveling alone through the desert, the darkened Pampa, for kilometers and kilometers back to the city. Sometimes, the young milico would tell us a story, and the gringo who drove the truck would laugh in his wide voice;

4

but that one wasn't a yanqui. It turned out he was Dutch, although he still spoke like a yanqui, and he had blond hair. The milico talked about his girlfriend who had hazel eyes, and the lady smiled, even though she was ill. Mamá told me to sing for a while, so I sang "Niña en tus trenzas de noche," Mamá's favorite song because it's about a country girl from the south of Chile, not from this desert, yellow at midday and reddish at sunset, with features that fade under the moon and the fog.

Since I am twelve years old, I like the desert, and the high altitude makes me feel very light, but Mamá gets puna sickness. The first time I went to the desert with Mamá, we passed along the side of a mountain in a village called Caspana, where the road was so narrow that the jeep barely fit, and Mamá told me proudly that the Indians of Caspana had built that stone road with their own hands. I was looking out the window at the side of the mountain, where the road seemed to have been cut straight down with a knife, and it occurred to me to ask, what would happen if another car came from the village? Would we have to back up? No one answered, but Mamá said, "¡Ay, niñita!"

We had gone to Caspana to speak with the school teacher, and he invited us to have breakfast. I remembered how good that breakfast was while I tried to fall asleep and couldn't hear anything, except the silence. I thought about the breakfast, about the mountain covered with flowers and icy frost at the same time, about the rocky pool in Toconao where I couldn't swim, but again I heard the truck rolling in the darkness of the Pampa and la señora in my mother's arms while I sang, "Niña en tus trenzas de noche, ¡ay, luceros de rocío! traes la risa mojada cantando al borde del río."

In Caspana, the river flows alongside the mountain in a very deep ravine. I was thrilled because I had never seen a ravine; even the name was an adventure for me. I went out to play with the school teacher's children and, when I told them of the other wonders I had seen, such as waterfalls in the south of Chile, they laughed, two boys younger than me. We started jumping over the rocks and climbing down the walls of the ravine. I was trying to get some wild flowers that had a thin, little stem. One of the boys said there were trout in the river, and when I looked down, I slipped on the ice, almost falling to the bottom. I was so scared I didn't even scream, but the boys yelled and scrambled in search of a branch to help me. With my dignity wounded, I climbed up the rocks until I reached the edge, and we got away from there.

The sun was shining in Caspana. There was a soft silence in the air. From the road, one could see the village encrusted in the mountain where the uneven houses seemed to have grown like that, one by one for a long time. Behind the houses were the cultivated terraces, barely sprouting green, descending gradually to where the irrigation canal opened. Beyond the houses and the reddish and brown earthen steps, the desert began.

The teacher took my mother and the others for a walk and told us how the leaders of the three political parties had come to say their speeches and to convince the people to vote for their candidate. The people listened respectfully. Each leader was very pleased and offered a huge poster of a pale and serious candidate. The teacher showed us where the posters were pasted up, one right next to the other, as if they were all the same.

In Caspana, as in almost all the desert villages, there is a little school with stone walls and dirt floor. All the houses are built the same way, but in the village of Toconao they are made of white stone, like its beautiful rocky pool. In Toconao, jumping along with one foot in and one foot out, I followed the stone aqueducts that were used for irrigation. They were dry in the summer, finally ending at an orchard of pear trees, very tall and heavy with fruit. The orchard was large and the pear trees were all lined up along the sand. East of the valley, I found myself surrounded by rock walls so tall that streams of water broke from the stone, watering the branches and ferns. It was all so pretty that I could hardly contain myself with delight. When I ran to tell Mamá, I tripped over a dead animal that looked like wild boar. I had never actually seen a wild boar like the ones in the jungles, so I was very excited by such a find, but Mamá said it wasn't a boar after all. It was just an old pig.

Everything is quiet. When I close my eyes I see the water, deep and crystal clear, that flows from a spring in the Loa river to form the rocky pool in Toconao. The boy who hasn't slept in four nights is very quiet; four nights awake, caring for his mother, until we arrived in Peine with the truck. He has finally tried to sleep, but la señora had been sick for a long time, and the people in the hospital first asked her to what political party she belonged. The people in the hospital are real beasts, that's what Mamá said.

We have made many trips into the desert, to the villages in the interior, looking for art work for the Fair in Calama. The people are amiable and calm. The kids are dark, with freckles like mine, and everybody speaks with a question at the end of their sentences. Mamá asks them about their crafts, the weavings and decorated pottery of brown and red clay. In Toconao, a young man named Emilio made a clay replica of his village church. It was very pretty, and it even had real bells on the top.

There was a lady with very long braids who wove cloth tapestries in multicolored patterns while she sat on the ground using her hands and her feet for a loom. Doña Guillermina had been in jail because she didn't have a birth certificate. She couldn't prove to the authorities that she was Chilean and hadn't crossed the desert from Bolivia, but when it came to voting in the elections, the authorities developed sudden blindness about the certificates, that's what Mamá said.

Emilio's mother told us stories about ancient times, about the people of the sun. She pointed to the sky, the bluest sky I have ever seen, where I imagined time floated, ageless. But there had been changes. She told us of the times before she was born when the rains came down faithfully to water the fields where the llamas and the alpacas grazed peacefully in the abundant grass.

In each village, we were welcomed by the teacher's wife. Later, we visited the church, but because of my age, I was always sent to play with someone, while Mamá talked and organized the Fair. When we went to Chiu Chiu, we visited the church built by the Jesuit Order in the 1500s. I didn't want to stay because it looked like a tomb, with low, yellow stone walls and narrow corridors. In the sacristy, there were purple cloths and lace, extremely old saints, and a virgin about a meter tall, dressed in velvet robes with a porcelain face, glass eyes and a gold crown. I had heard of the statues of the saints that the Jesuits used to convert the Indians. They were like that, with real hair and glass eyes that shed tears through pinholes under the eyes, or blood through the palms of the hands. Then the priests would declare it a miracle.

Around the jeep, a group of people had gathered, talking about the Fair. Mamá came down from the church with a group of young people who had decided to go to Calama in two weeks when the Fair was due to start. Mamá invited them to our house. A woman introduced the weavers and the craftsmen who made the pottery. As we were leaving, she gave us a loaf of bread which we ate on the road. I was so happy traveling with Mamá, always learning about new things. In the Pampa that is so big, there is no reason to be sad, with the sun and the gentle wind. Now, I am sad, but in those days, I just didn't know.

Today's trip was the longest. In Toconao we stopped just for a little while to pick up Emilio's church and place it carefully in the truck, wrapped in blankets of llama wool. Emilio sent his little sister to play with me and we went running, because she told me she would show me the pool. We ran along a path, when suddenly there it was, like an open eye that extended all around. There were crevices and cracks in the rock that let creeping plants grow through; some grew even under the water. The two of us lay down on the edge to look at the bottom of the pool where one could see all kinds of little stones, plants, and bluish little fish. I had never seen something so wonderful. The girl seemed to understand because we remained quiet, and didn't even tell each other our names. The water looked sunny and clear, full of color. It was almost impossible not to jump in and swim with open arms from edge to edge carved in yellow and white stone, warm against the cold water. The girl and I smiled at each other.

Before leaving Toconao, the young milico had to put more gasoline in the truck with a hose. Each time he sucked the air out of the hose and placed it in the gas tank, the gasoline flowed back to the barrel and nothing came out. I offered to help, but he said thanks anyway. The Dutchman, who turned out to be from the Salvation Army, began to oversee the business of getting the gasoline into the tank. Mamá talked with a lady who knitted woolen hoods. All of a sudden, the gasoline started to come up from the barrel and made the milico swallow a mouthful. He had to cough and spit behind the truck, but he didn't want anyone to worry about him.

We headed for Peine, which is the most remote village, nestled almost at the foot of the Andes. The road was long, and I fell asleep until we arrived. The Town Council was waiting for us in Peine with a variety of contributions for the Fair: multicolored mantas, thick blankets of llama wool that were a pleasure to touch, knitted ropes and bridles of alpaca wool that had been braided with a design in brown and black wool. The ropes were very strong, the only ones used to herd the animals. People wrote their names proudly on the list that Mamá kept, where it was indicated who owned which article and how much money would be received in case it was sold at the Fair.

At the teacher's house we were invited to eat. The teacher's wife was shy and didn't talk with the others, but I remember her because she was very pretty, tall and dark, with small hands and the smile of an angel. A young man sat on one of the wooden benches and played the guitar. It had been such a long day in the desert that I barely remembered my home. I would have stayed there forever.

Before we left, a man came to talk with Mamá by the truck. That was when I knew we would be bringing passengers to Calama, a lady who was sick, and one of her sons. She and the boy took the back seat next to my mother, speaking in hushed tones.

They say that nighttime in the desert is treacherous, because darkness comes suddenly and the temperature drops. When the truck started back on its way to the city, it was already dusk. I didn't worry about anything else. I cuddled up on one of the seats with a woolen llama blanket, looking out the little window at the road. I still have the sensation of being on the road, buzzing across the desert, hour after hour, remembering what I had done during the day, especially my little friend by the pool who had

10

asked me to come back. I had said yes, but I didn't know her name nor she mine.

Everyone was quiet on the truck. The young milico felt sick for having swallowed the gasoline, so he stretched along another seat. The boy was looking at his mother seated next to mine. I went to speak with Mamá and la señora coughed a little. Mamá took her hand, and she calmed herself. Her son told us that they had been trying to get to the hospital for days, but there was no one to take them. There were no cars in Peine because it was so far from the city. The previous week, a military truck had passed by, but they could not transport civilians. La señora nodded slowly. A jeep had also passed through, but the men who drove it said they were on political campaigns and could not go out of their way. Four days during which the lady could barely breathe.

It was already dark and it was cold. Mamá told me to sing something pretty. I sang a popular song that I liked, but it didn't sound right with the noise of the truck and everything. The milico felt better and asked me to sing a tango, but I didn't know any tangos, so he sang a bolero. Then he became nauseous again with the gasoline he swallowed and he had to lie down.

I sang "Girl with the braids dark as night", thinking about the words of songs, about the minerals in the desert, and so many things, that I didn't even realize it when the truck took a narrower road, full of holes. We were on our way to San Pedro de Atacama because la señora had gotten worse and we had to get to the clinic where there would surely be a doctor, or at least, the medicine she needed.

San Pedro is one of the best known villages, perhaps because of the museum, or perhaps because it's a little over two hours from Calama. But Mamá told me that San Pedro was the first village the Spaniards found when they crossed the desert. Pedro de Valdivia took the village, burned it, and killed twelve of its chiefs; then, he ordered a church to be erected on the site.

I remembered when we went to San Pedro for the first time. We went to see the archeological museum and to talk with the Belgian priest who had founded it. He was such an easygoing man that he didn't seem to be a priest, and he knew so much about the Indians in the Atacama desert. We saw mummies buried in huge clay pots, necklaces of polished turquoise, carved snuff tablets, and arrowheads of black stone. Since then, I wanted to be an archeologist to uncover tombs and learn the history of the desert.

Before reaching San Pedro, one has to pass between two mountains of pure salt. There, rock salt is obtained with dynamite, not excavated like the copper in Chuquicamata. After the mountains, there is a valley of sand dunes called *Valley of the Moon*. During the day, the valley is just part of the desert, but at night, the mountains of salt give off a whitish light, or perhaps it is the fog; crossing the valley this time everything had changed so much that it really could be the valley of the moon. I kept thinking about the surprising changes of the Pampa. Perhaps it was the salty atmosphere that produced the ghosts, because there were always stories about the souls of people that get lost in the Pampa and wander forever in the sand. That's why one can see along the road, all covered with dust, small altars with a little virgin and an inscription to commemorate the lost travelers.

Once in San Pedro, we went straight to the clinic. It was almost midnight, and we were cold to the bone. Mamá and the Dutchman ran to speak with the nurses and look for the doctor, but there wasn't a doctor on duty that night nor any way to find one. Along the cold tile floor the nurses brought a stretcher for la señora, and took her to an emergency room to give her oxygen.

12

No one spoke to the boy, even though it was his mother. We were left waiting in the hallway while Mamá went to call Calama so they would be ready to see la señora at the hospital.

The milico whispered to me that the doctor was in the city, and I asked him why there wasn't an Indian doctor who could always be at the clinic. "Eso mismo", said the milico. I said I was going outside to pray to the Virgin.

Now, the night is still, and I don't want to shut my eyes in the darkness. In the morning, Mamá will say that la señora passed away last night, her voice drifting like the sand on the desert, and my questions, all my many questions, will be stuck in my throat.

Looking out the back window, I could see how the truck overtook the distance minute by minute. Whispering the words, I prayed to the Virgin to save the lady, to shorten the road, to make the lady breathe, sleeping in short spells in my mother's arms, but I didn't pray to the virgin of the Jesuits. It was a virgin that I had invented, a virgin dark and alive who rose out of the beautiful rocky pool in Toconao, a virgin full of light spreading all over the desert.

While we were still on the road one could see black shadows that looked like folds in material, and every time we passed over one, I prayed with all my soul that the Virgin would use the fold to shorten the road. Barely moving my lips, I repeated "Let it shorten, let it shorten," like a magic formula, trying to find all the faith I had until the distance really was overcome and one could see the lights of Calama. In the back seat, Mamá said "*Fuerza señora*, have strength, we are almost there." The lights got closer, and from time to time a small house appeared, and a truck, a bus, then another house, another, and I happily praying, secretly, until we got to the hospital and some orderlies came out with a stretcher for la señora. I said goodbye, "*hasta luego, señora*, hope you feel better." We all followed behind the stretcher but we had to wait again in the hallway. There we stayed, the Dutchman, the boy, the milico, and I, looking at the yellow tiles until we saw a doctor go by, then a nurse and then nothing else for a long time. Finally, Mamá came out and said to the boy that we had to get in touch with his aunt as soon as we got to our house, and that his mother would be better in the morning. The boy said thanks and we got on the truck again. That was when she whispered to the Dutchman that they still had not cared for her, that they asked her what political party she belonged to, and Mamá was very angry.

It must be four in the morning and it has been a long time since the phone rang with the call from the hospital. Everything is quiet and when I close my eyes, I see the road in shadows that shorten and shorten but, ¡ay! la señora has already died, saying hardly a word to anybody.

❧

milico: any man in the military; here, a young private.
"Niña en tus trenzas de noche," a folk song by Clara Solovera, begins, "Girl of the braids dark as night, ¡Ay! Stars of dew! Your laughter rings wet from singing along the river's edge."

14

By the time his first granddaughter was six, he had painted every day of his life. From the time he was fifteen, he carried a sepia-toned pencil, a gum eraser, a handful of camel hair brushes and some tubes of paint, an old wooden pallet with a hole for his thumb, a jar of turpentine, and whatever surface he could find handy when the inspiration struck him. In those days, kicking around the gracious old streets of Santiago, he was a young man with aspirations, poor, but genteel.

In fact, the brushes and the oil painting had not come until much later, when he had sold a few portraits and could afford to buy his own oils rather than *borrow* someone else's. Still, he always thought of himself as carrying these things around with him as long as he could remember.

He sat down in his daughter-in-law's comfortable living-room, in the small and clean apartment where his only son, the middle child of four sisters, lived with wife and daughter. He felt at ease, there. He was hungry, but he knew that soon he would be eating a very tasty and nutritious meal. He sniffed the air and wondered briefly why he didn't yet smell the aromas coming from the tiny kitchen where his daughter-in-law must be busy at this moment cooking him a meal.

His granddaughter played quietly next to him, showing him her drawings, chattering about something unimportant, surely. He would pay attention later. Perhaps he would tell his wife all about his visit when he returned home, and his wife would listen to him, her wide, patient brown eyes resting on his face, the same look he'd grown accustomed to for thirty years. The little girl at his knees was staring up across the little red-tiled patio and he followed her gaze. His daughter-in-law was approaching, walking measuredly, carrying a tray. He settled back in his chair, preparing himself simultaneously to enjoy the delightful meal with his loving family and to unconvincingly pretend he wasn't really expecting to partake of any of it. He was preparing for a ritual he'd always enjoyed, the one when he refused and protested. As kind friends insisted that he must nourish his creativity as well as his body, and they inevitably prevailed on him, he would eat hungrily, surprising everyone with his voracious appetite.

This time he was the one surprised. There was nothing on the tray but tea and toast. Embroidered napkins were neatly folded, pretty porcelain cups, tastefully arranged pieces of toasted bread smeared sparingly with butter and marmalade. He noticed these details, challenging himself to imagine an oil rendering of the domestic scene, but he felt little inclined to continue the exercise, indeed to put on any of his usual performances for the benefit of such a meager offering. His granddaughter respectfully waited until her mother encouraged her to begin. His daughter-in-law then set a cup for him on the arm of the chair. She asked him about his wife. She told him that his son was still unemployed, even though he didn't care about that. That wasn't what interested him at the moment, until he realized that there must be a connection between the poor tea being offered and this news about his son's job.

His daughter-in-law and his granddaughter each took a piece of bread, and he stared at the plate, now suddenly like a still life, as it grew smaller, much smaller once the two pieces were taken from it. He took a piece himself, ate it, drank tea, took another, and envisioned himself as an oil of a grandfather, wearing an old suit, his hair gray, his shoes scuffed, desperately in need of a hot meal. Smiling and laughing softly he indicated his hunger as he continued to eat, the portrait in his retina taking in the understanding nods of his daughter-in-law and granddaughter, and their quiet encouragement to take another piece, more sugar, the last piece of bread.

Satisfied, he leaned back once more and benevolently accepted his daughter-in-law's apology. She had not realized how hungry he must have been, but that was all they had. Now it was his turn to nod in agreement and smile again, and play with the child while the mother saw to the cleaning up, such a clean little home she ran. His granddaughter's brown curls reminded him of his own children, now grown, of course, but two of his baby daughters had died when they were much younger than this— two or three years old, perhaps— when they lived in those southern towns, Lonquimay, near the border with Argentina, Osorno, near the volcano. One from diphtheria, and the other? Some childhood fever had taken the little angel. He should have painted more portraits of them. How sad his wife had been, inconsolable for a long time, and it was hard for him, traveling as he usually was, from art fairs to other opportunities back in the capital to develop his art. He would sketch his grandchild now, here, on the cardboard back of this drawing pad someone was

17

using, his daughter-in-law? Yes, it was possible. His daughter-in-law had mentioned something about working with pastels, water colors... quite interesting. Ambitious for a woman.

The child sat quietly while he sketched in sepia and rendered a beautiful, round-cheeked cherub to leave off-handedly on the back of the drawing pad. The mother would find it later and thank him warmly another day. How used he was to having grateful parents thank him for these sketches. It was a pleasure for him, and so simple to do.

That is why he was so surprised when his daughter-in-law came back from the kitchen and angrily snatched the child away, tears in her reddened face, ignoring the drawing he had just finished with an expert stroke of his well-worn sepia pencil. He walked home in silence. There was something he didn't understand.

❧

Today, because it is one of those strange winter days that is deceptively cold yet looks like a warmer day, I decided to open the small bag of harina tostada. Nothing more than toasted flour from my country, but wrapped as it was in a brown paper bag as well as a tattered plastic cover to keep the bugs out, and stashed away in a corner of my refrigerator, it looks like something I'd buy off the back of a truck, something rationed, hard to get.

It's been years. I'm an old man. That's how it is with these things we do out of nostalgia. The sky is light blue and the clouds move imperceptibly, laced with sun. I know it's cold out there on the street. Amsterdam Avenue is quiet for a moment. I have the bag here, and finally, I cut a corner of it to pour out a small amount of the precious stuff into a bowl. I got the small bag of flour from another guy who'd recently gone back to my country and brought back strange things like this. Toasted flour. Dried mushrooms. And those famous Chilean mussels canned in brine that are so cheap over there but cost a fortune here. I just bought the flour.

Of course, it sent me spinning back to the old neighborhood, near la estación central, when it was winter in Santiago and a bunch of kids from down the street and I would sit together on my neighbor's doorstep eating our breakfast of toasted flour ulpo. Who knows why we liked to eat it like that, all together, the cups steaming into the cold air. I remember the pasty taste of the hot flour mush dissolving on my tongue, the taste of the milk and the lumps of sugar that hadn't quite melted yet. And the kids, all snot-nosed, my nose probably running, too, but I don't remember that. Then, my grandmother would come to the door and shoo us all off to school, indulgence in her voice, but annoyed, as if we had done something wrong by sitting around like that, eating breakfast outside of our homes, a bunch of boys with our hair still wet but not very clean, on a winter morning in 1949.

Now, I prepare my breakfast in a bowl, not a chipped cup, and I use skimmed milk after stirring in the boiling water into the flour. The comforting lumps start to form; my mouth waters, I feel myself spin into the past. I add just half a teaspoon of sugar and a couple of dried figs from California. It's not exactly the same thing but it does the trick. I bring the bowl with me to stand by the window, lean against it, look outside. My clarinet case makes a good place to put the bowl down for a moment, while I adjust my glasses, take a breath. I brush off a little of the dust from the stand up bass I learned to play, years ago, because of a friend. Then I put the bowl on the piano next to all the sheet music I keep revising for my favorite students, kids from the neighborhood. The clarinet case is old, reinforced leather, and has a small bronze plaque on it that for some reason I never had the chance to get engraved with my name. It's a fine instrument, an antique I bought once in Milan, and I've played it ever since, all my playing days.

It's this odd sense of eating a bowl of this stuff that brings that other memory into view. I'd been thinking about it, ever since I bought the bag of flour, but I didn't want to bring those people back to my heart again. It took years to forget them. Why call them back?

I was only twenty, twenty something when I left Chile with my clarinet thinking the world awaited me, which was the only way to do that, after all. I left the neighborhood which had become too small for me, my grandmother whom I'd never see again, my mother, my sisters, and my uncle with the wooden leg who thought he knew more about why I was going than I did. But I was young. I had ideas, and I knew more than anybody, so I left.

It wasn't that I thought I played so well, I knew it would take me years to play with the ease I craved, but I thought I had time to spare, so I signed up with a band, a raggedy ensemble playing jazz at all-night boîtes as they were called. We took a train north, which was stupid, because we only had to go back to Santiago to get on the cargo plane to Europe, but we were stupid. What else can be said. The thing is, we did make it to Europe, first to Hamburg where we starved and I got sick for the first time, drinking beer morning noon and night. It was the cheapest thing, and if you kept drinking it, my friends told me I wouldn't feel the hunger and I wouldn't mind the cold while we walked from gig to gig, at night, playing two hours here with some group, two hours there with some smoky-voiced chanteuse just as hungry as we were.

I can't remember some of the guys now, but I'll never forget kid-face Jaime who was lost in the final sweeps of Pinochet's secret police, and skinny Jorge who fell in love in Brazil and never went back. The two of them and I hopped on the train to Romania one night following a German guy who'd been there and said there was an excellent opportunity waiting for us. It was a jazz band led by a "negro" man who was a virtuoso, a man who was a messiah, who wanted to unite the world through music and was creating a band with musicians from all the world, all races, all sounds. This seemed like what I'd been waiting for my entire life, so I talked them into going with me. It wasn't hard. For us South Americans, so far then from a chance to hear anyone remotely as talented as our heroes, the greats of jazz, meant the world. When we got to Romania, the German got a better job, and the band leader had gone, deported, some said, because the authorities had learned that he wasn't a gifted artist from America, but just some French black guy who could speak English and blow the horn like Bird. In those days, we didn't know that governments could do things like that; but then we learned for sure that our visitors visas meant little, that we had to play while we could.

In Bucharest, the nights were colder than in Hamburg but the pubs were friendlier, though the beer wasn't cheap. The three of us were lost. Between us, we could play clarinet, alto sax, and drums enough to scrape a bowl of soup at the end of the day for each of us. We had lost the fat we'd brought with us on our bones, and we were starving. Gone were grandmother's cazuelas and my mother's empanadas that I used to disdain. I remember I was standing in front of a coffee house, almost fainting as I watched the cream on the pastries on their way to the rubicund children of a blonde woman. I was dreaming of how I would seduce her and demand that she feed me cream and berries before I satisfied her hunger in a silk bed, when the young Romanian spoke to me. A young man with black hair, wearing an old tweed jacket which I remember was such a contrast against the pink marble tiles of the coffee house. I was dizzy; he held my arm.

This guy, Sergei, was a genius, we thought. First of all, he gave us soup at his mother's house, around the back where his aunt took in laundry and probably saved our lives. Then he told us of his plan. He'd heard us play in a couple of dives and thought we had something; he played the guitar, he was in love with the guitar! He was a funny guy, short in stature, intense. He spoke a little of everything-- Spanish, Italian, Russian, German, and he and the neighborhood where his family lived looked so ordinary to me, they could all have been South American, except for the language, and the food. Maybe they were very different from me, but at that time I wanted to be rescued by something familiar, and so they were. This guy had been trained as a classical musician. He could play Bach or flamenco guitar in a concert hall, but there really weren't any jobs. He taught the children of the rich, where his aunt washed their clothes, and at night, he worked in pubs, cleaning, serving beer, playing a gig now and then. He loved jazz as much as we did.

He put our quartet together, taught us songs we'd never heard, called them standards, and encouraged us to think about other instruments, diversify. He told us we were going to the Soviet Union to play there because the communist party frowned on musicians who played music from the west, and so the only jazz grudgingly permitted was the one brought by foreign groups, and jazz was precious. The party didn't persecute foreigners so much, he said, and we were foreigners. We would be famous, eat well, have women following us around. We practiced in the laundry, late at night. He played licks as though he was pouring water, while the three of us tried to follow. I think now about how we managed to believe each other, how we could ignore the life around us. I still don't know, except we were young and we didn't see hunger when it wasn't gnawing in our bellies, and this guy played like an angel.

"Where's our first stop?" I asked him finally, when we had a few songs worked out and thought we would work our way from country to country.

"We're going to the heart," he said. "Moscow. We're jumping on the train at 2 a.m. Make sure you don't break your legs when we jump, or get sucked under the wheels."

The bowl is still warm in my hands, empty, the remains of the ulpo already dry. On Amsterdam, down on the street, a guy is setting up a three-card-monte stand. I don't know why he starts so early. It's barely eight o'clock. On a block where the sale of drugs moves as smoothly as the sale of bread fruit or bacalao, who does he expect to snare with his artifice of quickly moving hands and playing cards, at this hour of the morning? I once thought only tourists got caught in those games, but I've seen people from the neighborhood lose a twenty in the flip of a wrist. I've decided to anchor the bowl on the window sill and lean over to watch life awakening on the street while I wait for my first student.

It's not as if the street has been quiet all night. It's still winter. The light is slow in coming, and it was only an hour ago that the night people went to bed. These are the day people. The grocer across the street is pulling out the crates with produce from the Caribbean, while his neighbor at the shoe repair shop rinses the sidewalk clean of the excesses spilled last night on that very spot. The woman at the dry cleaners just sent her son out to sweep. Instead, the boy has gone to the grocer's and is helping the old guy set up the yautías in a box.

24

I remember when he first opened up, years ago. He brought some vegetable or fruit from everywhere in Latin America and the Caribbean, some teas, some special hot sauce or a spice that only certain noses would hunger for. That's how he got each of us, for blocks around, to come and shop. With memories. A little contraband we could compare from Chile to Trinidad. Oh, yes, my grandmother used to make that dish, the same way, yes, there's nothing like it. Wise old man.

In the Soviet Union that was then, there were people lining up for everything, everyone just as hungry as we, with a little money to buy from empty shelves. My old grocer would have done well over there in those days. He would have figured out what Soviets liked to eat, to smell, to remember from their childhood in Minsk, Georgia, or Azerbaijan.

That's what our new comrade, Sergei the Romanian, taught us to do before we left. In his mother's house, he took us to his little room where he packed, guitar, underwear, a sweater, and a large paper bag with a jar inside, full of crumpled bills and coins. To this, we added all the money we'd managed to save over the last few nights of midnight to dawn gigs.

We followed Sergei, sticking to his heels, Jorge, Jaime, and me, as he led us to an old district buzzing with commerce, cobblestoned and narrow, to the loading door of a factory. Sergei took the jar out of his paper bag and emptied it into the leather apron of a boy with a nose red from the cold who sniffled, and winked at us as he counted the money. We proudly spent our entire collective fortune on socks, black and gray men's socks.

"This will be a luxury over there, you'll see. We'll be able to eat and play. Let's go."

In retrospect, my heart beats along the edges of that memory, remembering how kind the Romanian was, willing to share everything he had with us, and we, who were so young, accepted his kindness without a word. Jumping the train wasn't easy. We could have died, each one of us, but we pulled and grabbed, scrambling with the strength one can only have at twenty-one. Frightened and elated, we slept all the way across the border, drinking vodka, so we wouldn't have to eat. Jaime laid his head on the paper bag full of socks, closed his eyes on his big kid's face, and kept it safe.

It wasn't until we'd gotten there, to the formidable Moscow on the edge of Spring, stashed our instruments in a little hotel that accepted Jorge's drum set as collateral and got an egg and a piece of bread each as part of the bargain, that I realized we'd have to work even harder to keep our wits about us, more than we ever had before. Jorge caused a scene and threatened the manager with his skinny arms, if anything happened to his precious drums. We dragged him out of there, swearing revenge in some English and German he'd picked up.

"Don't worry," Sergei told Jorge about the drums. "The place where we'll play tonight has a set of drums, and by tomorrow, we'll have enough to get yours back from the hotel."

"Ha, I'm not worried," Jorge told him, mostly in Spanish, which is what the Romanian seemed to know best, although it came out sounding like Italian. "The skins broke when we hopped the train; anyway, I was gonna play Jaime's sax and show him how it's done!" On the streets, people were starting to mill around, St. Petersburg rising impossibly movie-like behind us as we talked.

"Be my guest," Jaime told him. "I've been thinking of learning how to play the bass."

"Do you Chileans ever stop joking?" Sergei cuffed the two of them on the head and directed us to a good spot on the sidewalk.

The sun was breaking through. It was Saturday. Soviet citizens heard about a new shipment of meat and were lining up. An old woman was selling garlic from her apron. A man had two harmonicas to sell. Sergei opened the paper bag and took out two pairs of socks

A thousand pigeons lifted in flight towards the cupolas and a swirl of men and boys approached us. In a matter of minutes, I became a broker, along with Jorge and Jaime, for the greatest sock sale of the century. People threatened to form a circle around Sergei, which would have been too obvious for the police, so we dispersed, selling here and there, among the garlic and the odd bar of soap. People shoved rubles at us, coins, bills. Some spoke whatever language they thought we did, or not at all. The socks were going fast. The faces of the people became mine, a memory, a grandmother's face, an uncle, and strangely, I thought, would I ever go home? Is there home anymore? And why, why on earth did I ever think I knew where it was?

I can still see the path from Red Square to the hotel. The four of us walking nimbly away, the paper bag empty. Three of us trying to breathe in unison with Sergei, thinking we saw a raincoated agent following us as we turned the corner, affecting nonchalance, passing newstands, the huge department store named Gump's, the bridge, the Hotel Budapest, and then our small hotel. We had money to eat, I knew, and to sleep in the hotel, but for now we were unconcerned, letting Sergei take care of everything. I collapsed on one of the two beds and closed my eyes, listening to Sergei telling Jaime and Jorge to get some sleep before the gig we'd play. "I heard of an even better place, he said, and they have a new drum set."

"Can't sleep!" Jorge and Jaime were wound up. "Going to go see the tombs of Lenin and Stalin. And a museum. And buy vodka for a Russian girl!"

I sat up, but only half way, laughing at them because none of us knew anything about politics, much less Lenin or Stalin. Jorge only wanted to go so he could impress women, I knew that. Sergei threw a bunch of coins on the bed for them, and waved them on, untying his shoes and carefully placing them under the bed.

"Come back at eleven tonight, and be awake!"

No sooner had we closed our eyes than we heard a knock on the door, and someone rattling, turning the doorknob.

"The agent! The police!" I whispered. Sergei and I jumped up.

I can't believe how absolutely calm the Romanian was back then, and by example, so was I. We could have been dragged away, jailed, lost, deported, who knows. Who would have known? From the safety of my perch above the avenue, that day seems so distant but, at times, when I see my neighbors on the prowl for a special aguardiente or spices and flavors from home, I wonder. It's all so close. Sergei opened the door, then, to let in a young man, wearing a raincoat and a five-day growth on his gaunt face. It was the same man I'd seen following us on the street, but I knew then he wasn't an agent, he was one of us.

He spoke in Russian, I assumed, and Sergei shook his head, showing him the empty bag, telling him before his earnest protests that we had no more socks to sell, no more, they were gone. The man looked at me and spoke, making gestures, then turned to Sergei, his palms up, smiling, his teeth yellow, his eyes brown.

"He has a date," I told Sergei. "Tonight, he has a date with a girl and he wants socks!" The three of us bent down and looked at the man's ankles, bare and white, stuck in shiny black shoes. Sergei looked at me and the man looked at Sergei, at me, finally at Sergei again and pointed down at his feet. In a silent conversation that perhaps can pass only among men, Sergei protested that his own socks wouldn't do, they were worn, dirty, after all, but the man needed them. I nodded at Sergei, who went to the sink where he took off his black socks and rinsed them out. My own would not have done, as they were blue with a black stripe and had holes in the heels and toes. I wiggled them at our visitor so we could chuckle softly, man to man, while Sergei wrung out his socks in the sink. He gave them to the man who thrust bills and coins at him, but Sergei pushed him away.

Greedily I raised my eyebrows and tried to convince Sergei to take the money, but he sternly shook his head and told me to lead the man to the door. I did as he said and escorted our visitor away from the sink while Sergei dried his hands. As I opened the door, the man embraced me, whispering his thanks in a husky voice, to which I responded as huskily as I could, in my own language. And he slipped the money in my hands before I closed the door behind him. I didn't stop him. I heard the man run down the stairs.

I knew Sergei would be angry, that he wouldn't want to hear me, but look, I persisted. We need the money, we can stay longer, play another gig, we need to eat. Sergei sat on the bed and shook his head, smiling sadly at me. He seemed old, though I knew him to be only a couple of years older than I was. I sat next to him and shoved the money in his hands. He let it drop on the floor and tussled my hair.

My footsteps sound tired to me nowadays, I can imagine what I must look like to the young people in the neighborhood. The young Jamaicans, the Dominicans, the Ethiopians sweeping the sidewalk in front of their restaurant next to the Colombian coffee shop. I place the bowl in the sink and run some water to fill it, scrape at the crusted flour with my thumbnail. Even my fingers are old now.

We didn't get famous in Moscow or in Budapest where we stopped weeks later, but we played the best jazz imaginable, the best that could be had for the few coins those young people had to offer, crowded in the smoky basements, listening intently, tapping along with Jorge's cymbals, their eyes misty or sharp, laughing, or talking seriously, girls dancing together, boys flinging arms over comradely shoulders, couples sneaking kisses under the shadowy stairs. Their applause was thunderous, always, their arms always hardy when they embraced us and took us among them to feed us breakfast at two in the morning, three, four, before going to work, to school. We dragged ourselves across hazy Moscow streets to our hotel room to sleep senseless, until evening.

Through the window of that little hotel room, I saw what happened. Look, I said to Sergei; it's the sock man. Sergei shoved me aside and drew the curtain across the window, leaving only a narrow slit through which we could see. Down below, two burly men had grabbed our visitor, had stripped him of his raincoat and were searching him with their big paws. He was thin, couldn't have been older than we were. He was shoved into a car, incongruously a light blue boxy car that could barely fit the two gorillas who grabbed him, or so I thought. I looked at the money on the floor and thought of the girl who'd be waiting somewhere, maybe even at the place where we'd play, that night. I couldn't look at Sergei, but when I did, he was sleeping.

By nine thirty this morning, my best student will be here, Zoraida the clarinetist, a Puerto Rican girl from the Lower East Side who hates her name, has thin fingers and big ideas.

"Your name will not make you famous anyway; play your scales."

"I don't want to play scales, maestro. I want to play jazz, go on the road like you, be famous and change my name to Zed!" She plays a riff of her own invention, and I don't respond, standing by the window where I can smile in private. Zoraida plays her scales.

I went on the road, it's true, for years, and by the time people in small towns knew my name, alone or with a quartet, it had ceased to matter. By then, I had the road in my blood, where the music coursed, relentless. Time passed, and I went back, to Chile, to the many places there were to go back to. That's how I knew Jaime was dead, he and how many thousands of others. I saw the block where my grandmother lived until she died, where we sat, five snot-nosed kids eating our toasted flour in the winter mornings. It was smaller than I thought, shorter, the street narrower and sadder than I could ever imagine. None of the guys from back then was around anymore, maybe that's what made it sad.

Jaime went back to Europe with me once because Jorge left the group on a tour of Brazil when he fell in love. We left him in Bahia, fat, happier than we'd ever seen him before. "Send my best to Sergei," he yelled to us as we hopped a train. And Jaime, when we parted ways, pressed me to find Sergei again, to tell him all we'd learned over the years. "Tell him that I learned to play the bass."

31

But it was years before I found the old street where his family lived. Sergei had disappeared, too, had been arrested one day during Ceaucescu when he was teaching guitar at a school, never heard from again. I cried when I heard this, not for him because I knew he would not be bitter over his own death, but for me, for Jaime, for all the people who would never hear them play. I'm not so old, really, but if I am, this is why. My footsteps sound heavy to me when I walk.

Sergei and I did go see the tombs of Lenin and Stalin back then, looking perhaps for the sock man, hoping to see him free and walking about, maybe to invite him for a drink, to hear us play. There were hardly any people in the cavernous hall, their hushed voices echoing. I remember my friend's dark head and his gaunt looks, his nervous guitar fingers signaling me ahead, and then we saw. Stalin's remains had been removed because he had been denounced by the party just that day. The tombs were closed.

Sergei stood and read the signs to me, trying to make sense of what this meant, this huge indictment, this recognition of change. "Who knows what will come next," he mused, his eyes blinking fast.

I admit, with all that I've traveled, I don't understand much of the world. I'm not a smart man, just a musician. I have seen great things in little towns, and missed revolutions just because I've missed a train. I've lost instruments along the way, and got them back again. Once, traveling in Ecuador, I lost all my luggage, but got it back when I got to Guayaquil with a suitcase that didn't belong to me, full of oranges from Perú. These are the stories Zoraida and the others like to hear, and the ones about the concerts in glittering music halls or under tents in the rain. And I could tell her about the clarinet leaning over there, about

Sergei's jar full of coins and wrinkled bills, or why I play the bass, but she has no time to hear me.

Today, though, when she leaves, she'll carry two cases with her. One will be a very fine leather case with an antique clarinet inside, with a bronze plaque newly engraved with her name, *Zed*. At least, I hope she will, she may not want all these memories passed on from an old man, but maybe, maybe she will. And she'll play jazz.

❧

Marisa

Every city must have a river, a river like this, with cemented banks and bridges aglow by the street lights. . . dirty brown waters that don't look so brown when the city is in full bloom. But, look! Now it's a live Stieglitz in the rain. People with umbrellas walking on the sidewalks. In the Spring the scene is a Van Gogh, craft fairs, art exhibits, flowers, balloons, bright colors sliding from one brush stroke to the other. . . look down, now. See the waifs, the hoodlums. La clocharde de Cortázar, who inhabits the banks wrapped in newspapers, an eternal picnic, sordid little fires, heating tea in a can. . .

Marisa shook her head, shook her visions off, shook the water off that had pillowed in her hair as she stood by the river in the rain. She walked toward the diminutive cafe that looked steamy and warm in the late afternoon. Inside, she used her scarf to soak up the rest of the water from her hair. She placed her hands on the cold surface of the marble. With a still damp finger she traced the green swirls on the little table, looking up as if in a dream to the face of the older woman, to ask: "té con leche, por favor, y unos mantecados."

She felt frail since being released from the jail that wasn't a jail, from the arrest that was never an arrest, and surviving the experience she must never mention again. Miraculous. Her release was miraculous, owing to friends she didn't know she had, her survival and everything that surrounded her now, like new life in a new body, although vulnerable, and unused to the new curtness of people under curfew. The woman returned with a generous cup of steaming tea and a plate with three mantecados, freshly baked.

Marisa always put a whole one in her mouth. The thick, round shortbread pastry rolled on powdered sugar filled her mouth, and it was a test each time to conquer its sweet dryness without letting on that it might be too big a mouthful. It was a childhood habit of taking that deliberate walk to the mysterious shop near the school to buy one mantecado. It meant squeezing through the wrought iron gates of the school with the younger girls, the steady formations of little girls in white dusters over their uniforms, with only a few extra minutes to buy the mantecado, to run back to the bus, meeting the girls from her own grade, and to sit, triumphantly, with a mouthful bursting with powdered sugar, reaching for the crumpled hankie in her pocket, catching the inevitable cloud of laughter and sugar.

Marisa reached for the small napkin and wiped her mouth. Outside, the rain had stopped and the steady stream of umbrellas began to close their inverted petals, revealing their pedestrian stems. Marisa allowed one more reverie.

She stood at the gates of the school on a rainy afternoon. Sixty fourth graders surrounded her in neat files of five abreast. The gates opened and Marisa gasped. Around the stone steps, the parents had gathered in the most colorful array of open umbrellas, a semi-circle of flowers, striped and swirled patterns, enhanced by the rain on them. The girls swarmed around Marisa who awoke from her dream and took one last sip of tea.

On a plate by her cup remained two mantecados. There was something upsetting about eating more than one, more than one gobbled-up-one on the bus, on the way home from school when you're nine-years-old.

§

Raquel

Raquel rose late on Sunday. Having slept badly, she received the repetitive winter morning with resentful, tired eyes. At work at the embassy's kitchen the day before, she'd found out Marisa was alive. For eight months, she had mourned Marisa, based on the rumors around the embassy that the piano teacher had been arrested, tortured, and found floating in the river. At first, retaining in her mind the image of her unlikely friend, the piano teacher, with a whisper of a voice as she sang the scales with her pupils, the spoiled children of the consul, Raquel had refused to believe it. Until one day, like all the other disappearances in her neighborhood where people grew to accept them, Raquel accepted that Marisa was gone. No mourning anymore. Merely empty space in her gut.

When she saw the small Marisa, her dark hair in a braid draped over her shoulder, Raquel knew it was one of those things one keeps quiet, that this is how it's done in one's small, remote country. One does not react. She was sitting alone on the piano bench, then rising to kiss her good night on Christmas Eve, and timidly slipping the silky green package into her hands, she said, "For you, Raquel, open it after midnight."

Marisa was alive, and she still knew nothing about her. Raquel wiped the steam from the kitchen window and gazed outside, where her little sister played with her kittens. Unable to forget her dreams, mysteriously suggestive dreams about Marisa, she closed her eyes.. Raquel had turned over and over in her narrow bed in miserable wakefulness, but images invaded her tired body, more like threads of visions: scenes of a room furnished in dark wood appeared before her. She dreamed she waited with many people, young people, women like herself, in this room that looked like the embassy. Marisa sat before a dressing table. The milicos waited outside the door, pounding their rifle butts on the heavy wooden door-- "Tell that slut to hurry in there!" they yelled, and the other young women looked on avidly, while Marisa pulled jewels and silky things out of the drawers, pulling them off her own body, and handing them out, one by one.

Raquel turned over restlessly, half awake, half asleep, apprehensive, protective of Marisa, yet in curious alliance with the other women. Wearing a satin bodice, Marisa sat on a brocade stool. Light green satin, tightly fitting her body. She found a yellow pendant and handed it to a young girl who took it hungrily. Marisa's face remained impassive, her skin pale, chiseled out of a cold light. "More!" yelled the women, and Marisa pulled lace from curtains, from her own garment. Satisfaction.

Apprehension. With a kind of adoring hatred, an expectancy that bordered on desire, Raquel looked at the lace ripping, revealing more of Marisa's flesh around her tightly bound breasts. The pounding of the milicos, the greedy clamoring of the women, the rain tapping loudly on the windows. . . Raquel woke and remained cold, sitting up in her bed for a long time, trying to understand her dream.

Now she brewed tea mechanically. She imagined herself to be part of a black and white movie that contained a pot of steaming brown tea. She stood in the cold kitchen balancing her weight on the sides of her feet, not wanting to touch the cold tile floor. Warming one hand on the sides of the tea pot, she reached with the other into the pocket of her robe. Marisa's gift to her was there, the yellow topaz set in silver.

The screams of her sister Beatriz out in the yard brought her quickly to the window. Beatriz and a neighbor girl were coaxing two black kittens to board a makeshift boat floating in a puddle of rain water.

"Beatriz!" Raquel called her sister, "come over here, please!"

Beatriz looked up from her game. "Do I have to?" The two girls looked at each other in distress. "Hold these guys, Rosita, I'll be right back!" Forcing herself to look serious, Beatriz ran to the kitchen window, where Raquel expected her.

"Beatriz, what are you doing to those poor animals?"

"They wanted to go for a ride," answered the girl.

"But cats hate the water, silly! Let them go," said Raquel. Beatriz offered a dazzling smile, mirroring her sister's wide mouth, her high cheekbones, her shining black eyes: "That's why we put them on the boat, Raquel!" She turned swiftly, wasting no time to get back to the kittens. Returning to her pot of tea, Raquel told herself she must be appreciative of the wilfulness of the young, her sister and her friends, the boys in the neighborhood, for who else would live through this dictatorship, and flourish in the end?

§

Presentiment

She broke her fall on the tile floor with both hands, palms outstretched, and took the kicks to the kidneys in silence, lips tightening in panicked determination . . . checking, painfully lifting hems to apply cool fingertips to bruises, cigarette burns... her lower lip lapping tears, a runny nose and the thinner, saltier, blood . . . confirming in whisper that the woman next to her was also raped with electrodes (don't let them know you suspect what they might do, they cut me, the bastards) she spit out the words, a warning to Marisa, offering moist tea bags to soothe the burned skin, while waiting, waiting, knees turned to dough and still waiting . . .

Marisa shook her hair away from her face, her hand was captured again by Don Jorge, his kind eyes attempting to penetrate her own, murmuring concern. She pressed her face against his chest, pushing the memories away— why now? She could postpone the feeling of warmth her employer offered in the large room between the piano and the fireplace. She should close her eyes just like this and detach herself from his touch to be there, in that other place, remember everything over again, and feel nothing, nothing. Or she could open her eyes and be in her bed, absorb herself in the embrace of this kind man who had

39

saved her life, in tracing kiss by kiss the surface of his face, ignore the shock of intimacy as she would ignore the memories of that other place, and follow the feeling of her body being caressed without actually being there.

How did it happen? Did she sit too long by the piano after Raquel left, touching the keys lightly and knowing she had waited only for her to come, the notes reverberating against the vaulted ceiling, crying a little, perhaps, because she was so happy that Raquel knew? Was it when Jorge spoke her name in a question, the precise intonation, that her battered body turned, her face open to him, so glad to be alive. But then came his caress, his gentle kiss, her soft words wanting to end the mistaken preamble.

Released again from her thoughts, Marisa in turn released her hold of time and lay unmoving on her bed. Outside, the newspaper bundles hit the sidewalk, the metal doors rolled up and businesses came alive. In the distance, she thought she heard the purring of Jorge's gray Chrysler, but that could have been hours ago, when her eyes registered everything that happened to her in black and white, when she lifted her hands to her face again and felt it, wet with tears, and she heard her voice, very steady, sending Don Jorge away.

With the comfort of the noise outside her window, and the light streaming in, Marisa slept.

§

Fate

At the end of August the weather breaks. In the Plaza, magnolias burst open and birds sing in desperation, claiming a branch or the eaves under the round band shelter for themselves. But there is no

40

band. Old people are prohibited from feeding the pigeons because they will interfere with the general's parade. Children cannot be allowed to run, and dogs are out of the question. Mothers must perch a small tricolored flag on baby carriages. Preparations for September's festivities, the once raucous celebration of independence, are now carried out with unnatural order and decorum.

Braving the curfew, Marisa huddles in a doorway. She doesn't know where she is exactly. The neighborhood is not familiar to her. But this is the bus route that Raquel always took when she left her job at the embassy, it has to be the way. As light fades, the scent of eucalyptus grows stronger, and Marisa tries to take hold of her own steps, to root herself somewhere. Can she ever again trust a body that doesn't belong to her? She runs another block, deeper into the neighborhood where she sees lights, and vegetable gardens surrounded by cement walls painted pink.

An owl hoots, a human owl, giving the signal that there's an unknown pedestrian in the neighborhood. Teenaged boys run to peek out of doorways, to slide carefully along the sidewalk from doorway to doorway. Raquel joins the search as she hears the second owl hoot, indicating the stranger is friendly and unarmed. At the corner she sees the boys surrounding Marisa. She knows it's Marisa, her heart pounds out her name. The boys push the newcomer toward safety, toward any open door, and Raquel reaches for Marisa, taking possession of her body in this embrace, pulling her into the sanctuary of the darkened garden, murmuring thank yous and bless yous. The boys scatter, laughing nervously. The owl hoots three times.

෨

The fastest route to Maine, through New England, is plagued with the deadliest tourist traps. The journey is not so trying on those who stop, lured by antique signs and the like, as it is for those who don't stop and must watch carefully in front and behind for station wagons laden with families, slowing down and swerving off the road, left and right, at a moment's notice.

By the time I had reached northern New Hampshire, I was at a peak of exasperation. I had become a cycle of clumsiness and irritable outbursts over my own behavior, all of which made me fail in my attempts to drive calmly. I had been so accustomed to the maneuverability of my Ferrari, that driving this obscene, practically antique Ford was more than I could bear.

As I steered the big monster around a curve, I reached into the glove box where I had hastily thrown the case for my sunglasses and a package of French mints. I fussed around with the contents and instead of mints I drew out a small book of French poems. Disregarding all compulsion to be annoyed that the car had not been properly gone over before it was sold to me, I held the book in my hand instead, pleased, and bewildered that

I had a tangible memento of the previous owner of my Ford Galaxie. My preoccupation with the summer drivers faded. I turned the book over in my hand and discovered it was not of French but Canadian origin. Images of the past couple of days turned in my head, forcing me to recall the events that stranded me in Connecticut.

God only knows why I ever had the misfortune of incurring an accident in that miserable town, in the middle of summer yet, the sun beating hot, when I avoided hitting the old woman in the middle of the so-called Main Street. I swerved into the vestigial Pilgrim rock wall enough to burst my radiator, and there I was: sweating profusely, my Ferrari steaming profusely, the old woman thanking me profusely; it was a mess.

I was a mess, too, trying to figure out how to reach Maine before the weekend, while around me the townspeople said— with no attempt at decorum, considering the old woman who babbled in a daze— that I was a nice young man even if I did drive rather fast; at least I had wrecked my car just so I wouldn't hit old Miss... whatever her name was. Really! She had the perplexing habit of standing by the rock wall sweeping, sweeping I tell you, the dirt into the main road.

Well, not that any of that matters, really, though I was rather shaken. Still, I was to be shaken even more before I found a decent set of wheels that would get me to Bar Harbor.

Unlikely as it was, I found acceptable lodgings and was soon engaged in leafing through the local ad weekly in search of auto sales.

"1966 Chevy step van, paint job, 8-track, carpeted, runs. $500 or best offer." Really.

"1952 Ford pick-up, good suspension . . . " oh, God. And then, "1968 Ford Galaxie 500, carburetor trouble, $200." Well, then. Shall we give it a try. With minor adjustments, it might be just the thing to suit me until a new radiator could be procured for my Ferrari, and I could return to pick it up on my way back from Bar Harbor.

The annual bash at the big Cranberry Isle, off the coast of Bar Harbor, promised to be a delight. Only, the first time I was invited, I was more impressed with its prospects than I could ever be again. Why it seemed to me such a grand affair, I do not know. Certainly I had all I could desire of glitter, intellectual ladies, and smartly dressed boys— excitement, in a word— in the City. Yet, that coveted fortnight at the island had proved, in the previous two seasons, to be a sought-after relief for those who could travel at leisure through quaint New England, a sort of select twentieth century nobility, gathering oddities and amusing tales to present to our hosts. Intimate acquaintances the three of them. At any rate, I would do anything to avoid spending mid-July with Mother, Dad, and Aunt Elizabeth, sweltering in Windsor Locks, going inexorably from Church to Cotillion to Sunday horse shows. Oh, no. I longed to be free of my family, to hear our island hosts composedly receive our offerings from the road and regale us in return with champagne toasts and commiserations, such as John Michael whispering in my ear: "If only the sun would deign to shine upon us all year, you would never want to leave our side, here in our nook of the island . . ." or Imogene, prancing through the terrace, laughing, "Come, Gerard, come and dazzle these swarthy young sailors with your city ways . . ."

It was never established, actually, who was there to impress whom, because in our elite circle, no one ever *dazzled* lest it be by mere chance. And just how stupefied would everyone be when I had the nonchalant temerity of showing up at the Harbor in a Ford.

But, back to the matters at hand. The woman who was selling the car stood by, looking nervously now and then towards her house. I looked absentmindedly at the motor and forgot what I was looking for; she had so intrigued me. When I arrived, she had rather timidly gotten into the car and started it, while explaining that it usually stalled initially.

"It has a new starter motor, you see? The previous one kept disengaging; I believe it was loose. This one is alright, but I think there is something wrong with the carburetor. If you feather the gas pedal until it warms up, it should run well."

She wore her long dark hair tied back and had dark eyes that seemed to be constantly worried, until she became involved in explaining something. Then she seemed very young, until she looked towards the house again. She watched me for a while longer, as I looked over the car, as if she really could pay attention to what I said and at the same time keep track of whatever held her attention inside the house.

"Listen," she said finally. "I've got to go check on my son. Why don't you deliberate for a while and then come and tell me what you think."

I remember now that I enjoyed the way she had expressed herself. "Deliberate," she had said, with a slight inflection that was unusual for these rural environs. I wiped my hands with my handkerchief and decided to stop pretending I knew what to look for in a car. I followed the woman who'd already disappeared around the yard.

The door was open and I could hear, as I walked in, the end of a string concerto I recognized, one of father's favorites. I must admit I was surprised that I noticed at all, because I don't usually, but I noticed a small child sleeping in some sort of cradle in the front room. I sat down with a sigh, dutifully mourning my pleasures of the open road once more. Yet this time with less feeling as I got lost in studying the objects around me. I was not long into my new occupation when the woman returned carrying a child smaller than the first one I'd seen, and a look of inquiry on her face.

"Hi, well, what do you . . ." I interrupted her with:

"Is that? Well, how old is . . . they can't be twins?"

"Oh, no," she laughed a little. "This is my son; he's two months old. And that is my friend's daughter in the playpen. She is five months."

"Oh, you're baby-sitting!" I said, relieved, perhaps. She cuddled and kissed the baby as we talked.

"Yes, well. No, not really. It's just for a week."

We talked easily for a bit. Rather, I talked. I told her of my automotive misfortunes. I wavered between the pleasure of being appreciatively listened to and feeling extremely self-conscious talking to this woman who seemed to draw everything out of me while kissing and loving off-handedly the baby she held. As we talked, I remarked on the pleasant accent she had. She was Cree, she told me, from Canada. I told her it was unusual to meet someone like her in that part of New England.

"Or like you," she said. For a moment, I didn't know what she meant, what she had gathered about me. "This place is so odd," she continued. "It's nice to meet someone dark like you for a change; my baby and I are the only ones with black hair for miles."

She'd meant my looks, of course, my being black, which I hardly ever think about. I'd almost forgotten what I look like, and I certainly had forgotten about the car when she announced she would have to nurse the baby soon, and could I tell her if I'd made a decision yet? I mentioned something about talking to the mechanic at the corner station and returning immediately, when the other baby woke up with a start and a yell and had to be attended to. I realized then, due to her hesitation about my staying around, that she' really meant she had to *nurse* the baby, not just feed him a bottle.

I retreated awkwardly, suggesting I return that evening when her husband would be home, even though so far, I'd heard no mention of a husband or anything like one. She reassured me very kindly, with an amused smile and a baby in each arm. I don't know quite why, I was so shocked. Nursing babies. Really. I left the provincial menagerie soothing myself with the quaint story I would roll off the cuff when I got to the island ". . . nursing the baby, you know, mother's milk and all that."

I tried unsuccessfully to nap before dinner. I don't know why I was so tired. I examined my wardrobe with annoyance. Something that ordinarily gives me so much pleasure seemed exhausting then. The tan silk scarf with the beige denim slacks, the off-white muslin jacket. No, it would be chilly. I looked at my face in the small mirror on the dresser and wondered why I chose such muted colors. My tawny skin would look dull in beige. Why was I so partial to neutrals and pastels, as though I were . . . I forget who I am sometimes, and when somebody reminds me, it puts me in such a bad mood. What would I wear at the island in the evenings? It seemed I never had enough clothes while everyone else had just the right thing to choose from in their single suitcase. Finally, I abandoned this train of thought and snapped my suitcase closed.

Sitting on the bed, I gazed through the dark red shutters that opened onto the main road. For a moment, I imagined they framed the figure of my new friend, the woman selling the

Galaxie. What was her name? Emily. I pictured her walking on the beach wearing a bright, poppy-red sundress, holding a baby dressed in subtle turquoise and lavender. With her eyes, she followed the little girl playing in the sand, wearing a goldenrod playsuit. I felt absurd. I blinked away my fantasy and then recalled it with morbid pleasure to include the husband, a rotund little man dressed for golf in powder blue. I chuckled at my idea, imagining Emily straightening his collar and informing him that the car merely needed premium gasoline and a good dose of gum-out in the carburetor.

I closed the shutters, deciding then that I would simply be an hour earlier, would offer the fat plebeian of a husband $250 for the car, and drive it away that night. After a light supper downstairs in the pub and the inquiring glances of every soul in the place, I decided it was time. A foul cloud of exhaust enveloped me as I roared away in the town's only taxi cab to find my Galaxie.

When I returned to Emily's house, the car had been moved to the side of the driveway, and to judge by the bucket and rags lying next to it on the ground, it had been thoroughly cleaned. I knocked on the door feeling quite composed and prepared to carry the transaction out to a satisfactory conclusion that very evening. The door opened to a fragrant room, warmly lit by the evening sun, red peonies and yellow lilies in the corners, from where soft string music seemed to emanate.

Two hours later I sat comfortably, listening to my amiable companion, sipping the mildest mint iced tea, and having completely forgotten about the car I was buying and the husband (one did actually exist) detained by overtime. Emily's hands moved in a subtle dance as she talked. She would get up from time to time to bring tea or change a record, never altering the mood set by the previous piece, and to attend to the children who never stopped moving or making sounds of some sort.

The delight I took in listening to Emily had apparently been mutual. We shared great interest and similar opinions on music, food, literature, even clothes. She looked refined but comfortable in the emerald green, loose cotton pants and shirt she wore. Her figure was rather plump, yet this did nothing to detract from her agile movements. I couldn't really imagine the combination of her busy home life and the urbane demeanor she exercised. She spoke of her past travels, I spoke of mine. We laughed together at the pretentiousness of the haute bourgeoisie in my neck of the woods, both Black and white. She was enchanted by my tales of gay life in Manhattan.

"How can you bear the excitement, Gerard?" she said, almost to herself, and then turning to me, "If I were in your place, I would appear very bored at the sight of all the 'glitter', as you call it, just to reserve my energy to absorb it all."

"Yes," I laughed, "only someone with your kind of energy would be able to withstand the excitement of this coming weekend!"

When I saw that I'd puzzled her, I told her: "I'm being sarcastic, humorous, you understand. You are surrounded here by the most romantic, the most glamorous life," I waved at the flowers and the children.

"Perhaps," she said softly, and rose from her seat. Dusk shaded her face. She walked towards the playpen where one child lay asleep and the other threatened to wake him with her whining. Emily picked up her son. Then, her face, where anxiety was barely perceptible, softened. "But it's not always so glamorous, you know?" She cast her dark eyes in my direction. "I've got to put him to bed, and then . . ." she hesitated at the doorway. "Then I have to nurse my temporary daughter."

A very stupid smile must have been frozen on my face because, when she returned from the nursery, she opened her eyes wide and then explained.

"My best friend is very ill in the hospital. She can't nurse her baby for a week or more, and this baby happens to be allergic to cow's milk, or formulas. So you see, it is a very good thing that we are so close." Emily stroked the little girl's head. She sat in a big rocking chair holding the baby who nursed quite contentedly without my being able to detect how she managed it.

I was feeling out of my element, yet not entirely uncomfortable. Emily and I understood each other. But all this feminine mystery, and babies, and so forth. I tried never to be around babies; they were usually sticky and loud. It was getting to be too much for me. The music stopped, and I had barely tensed my muscles to get up and turn the record over when Emily detained me.

"Don't trouble yourself, Gerard. It's better for them without music for a while." I relaxed again, and after a silence so filled with thoughts, a comfortable silence I don't often experience, I gently returned to the subject of the car.

It would run quite well, she assured me. I would not be stranded again. A while later, both children asleep, I took my leave of Emily by shaking her hand longer than I needed to and trying to thank her for a kind of evening I could never explain to myself, nor its intense effect on me.

No more than the slightest hint of sea breezes had entered my consciousness, but enough to realize that my journey was almost at an end. The smell of summer roads and the lilies in

50

Emily's house were so distant now that the time I had spent there had the quality of dreamy fantasies I enter whenever I drive a long way. I could not help thinking about the way Emily had made me conscious of myself, because she seemed to really see me. And I could not shake the feeling that I had brought something to her life as well.

Soon, the noisy ferry would take me from the harbor to the island. With wistful relief at abandoning a subject that had turned too many times in my tired brain, I brought the stuffy little town to life once more: Emily, the flowers, the music, the babies, the multi-leveled conversations we had, and the bilingual nature of my mysterious friend— all were safely tucked away when I returned the book of French poems to the glove box of my Ford.

ఎ

She came to the City with her brother. She liked girls and so did he, which could sometimes be a problem. The first place they lived in was a room on Clinton Street, the cinnamon room, she called it, because the spice seller on the sidewalk below lived in the hallway, and he lent his many fragrances to the place. It would have been fine, if it weren't for the Mexican girl who stared at her brother while he worked on his drawings. The girl distracted him, asking him about life in Ecuador, always the same questions. What did you eat there, how big was your house. It was as if she wanted to move there with him, with Daniel, her pudgy, angel-faced and lazy little brother. Talented, but lazy. The only thing he was good for was drawing, imagining and sketching things, and the Mexican girl just wanted to marry her 19-year-old brother and go back with him to Ecuador, to Guayaquil, the city of soft colors, tropical and rich for others, not for orphans like themselves.

Serena didn't really mind that the girls liked her brother so much; he was a good brother and he wasn't lazy, just thoughtful. It was the way these young women always came around being her friends first, talkative, affectionate, admiring of her ability to earn a living for the two of them practically all by herself. And then, they saw Daniel. Quiet, talented, baby-faced Daniel, who didn't turn them away with brusque manners like the other men they knew, who didn't ask for anything and let himself be loved, while Serena was forgotten. Lithe, quick-witted, generous Serena. The same had happened in Guayaquil, and after Clinton Street, she wouldn't let it happen again. One pregnant girl trailing after Daniel was all they needed for their dreams to crumble.

It was their first summer in the City. They had arrived in February to look at a world enveloped in cold haze and gray rain. Taciturn inhabitants appeared to the two young immigrants like mole people, emerging somberly and resignedly from the malodorous subway caverns. The trees and the buildings had seemed to blend into the same bleak landscape, and when it rained and the trunks of the trees were soaked with cold rain, Daniel assured Serena that some plague had affected the country severely and vegetation would never return. But Spring had come almost unnoticed. Suddenly there were heady, sweet smells in the Park, the big park in the middle of the city, because Serena refused to spend their Sundays near the blighted park of Tompkins Square, and they would go off, wandering through the paths, getting lost, and finding their way out again.

She picked up their things one day, after sewing all morning at the clothing factory on East Broadway, and they moved. Daniel followed his sister obediently, never doubting that Serena knew what was best for them. This time, the move was to Elmhurst, in the borough of Queens, to share an apartment with a Chilean named Marcos and his American girlfriend, Nancy. Here, everything smelled like comino and fresh ink, from the pamphlets. Just for a few days, she said to them, to give her a chance to find another home for them. At last there would be no pubescent beauties staring at Daniel's long, straight eyelashes while he drew his fantastic creations on a sketch pad.

In unspoken exchange for a home, Serena helped Marcos to type and run off copies of Marxist pamphlets, while Daniel helped the girlfriend, Nancy, to make dinner. She was a very nice Black American, very committed to the cause, learning Spanish to help the Chilean movement in exile. Serena knew little about political activism, but she knew plenty about cooperation. She was a good comrade. She would have been a good guerrillera, Marcos told her, but she was here to make money. They left Elmhurst after two weeks, grateful, well fed with fried chicken and empanadas, and experts at stuffing envelopes. Serena had found a beautiful room in Manhattan.

Daniel touched the white window sills with his soft brown hands and looked in wonder at the plentiful sunlight pouring through the dusty glass onto the bare wooden floor of their large room on 103rd Street, five flights up. Drinking cheap wine and spreading out their blankets, tumbling out of a wicker basket all of Serena's new treasures, which they would use to build their future, he and Serena sat on the floor and giggled like two school children.

It was during a stroll along Broadway, since Serena would never take the train if she could help it, that they came upon the wholesale district near 28th Street. A new world opened, as they went from store to store and identified the merchandise that was later peddled in other parts of the city: leather bags, jewelry, crystals, toys, beaded clothes, sunglasses, socks. And although they were turned away by the *wholesale only* signs on the store windows, Serena found the ones that sold certain merchandise in small quantities. She bought crystals and beads, stones, cheap freshwater pearls, silver findings, nylon thread, and a special piece of Afghani lapis lazuli for herself. Her brown eyes twinkled with delight in a look of purpose that was familiar to Daniel. He knew she could make fantastic jewels with those hands of hers, and he chuckled softly.

While Serena strung beads and set crystals in silver wire, Daniel designed beautiful wood nymphs, llamas, Peruvian shepherds playing pipes, butterflies, exotic fish, dazzling hibiscus from his childhood in Guayaquil. Some of his ideas were things he knew; some were positively medieval and fantastic, things he'd never seen, but somehow the combination was wildly eclectic and very attractive. Serena varnished the figurines, drawn on shiny cardboard and cut out precisely to insert on the tops of pencils with a clasp. Daniel colored them with bright felt markers that she stole diligently from art supply stores. They had made an agreement that she would stop stealing as soon as they had enough money to live on, and then she would go to confession. Perhaps she could go find a priest at the big cathedral she'd found on Amsterdam Avenue, where she'd dragged a sleepy Daniel to look at the fantastic fountain with a sun and a moon, and a devil and crab's claws signifying something symbolic about peace. Daniel was properly impressed by the fountain, eerily illuminated by streetlight, and began to sketch on the spot on the back of a paper bag from Woolworth's.

The problem with Serena's necklaces and earrings was that everyone else in the City was making jewelry and selling it on the street in the summer. She invoked the patterns of the silversmiths in Quito, but it seemed someone else had already come upon the Native designs and brought them to Nueva York. Their wares sold slowly, but the hot noisy rooms of the clothes factory reminded Serena that she had to keep trying. In the afternoons, they would set up a folding table along Broadway, at Astor Place, or preferably in Soho, sometimes making a deal with the African sellers who were less concerned about the police or vending territory. Amin, the brass seller, traded Serena a smooth piece of amber for her lapis lazuli and told her the amber matched her vibrations, that she would *make things happen* with it.

One day, while sitting in the shade on St. Mark's Place, Daniel brushed his newly cut hair back and nudged Serena. Wrinkling her small nose she turned to him. On his hand was a miniature city made of cardboard, unpainted, but clearly depicting the shoreline of Manhattan, Brooklyn, Staten Island. Serena thrust out a disdainful lower lip.

"Look," whispered Daniel. "It bends here, and here. It can be attached to a ball, a sphere; it's a world."

"A globe!" said Serena, getting the point. The art work was painstaking, every minute detail of the portions of the City that they both had come to know were highlighted, the bridges, the Park, the Cathedral, the Twin Towers.

Customers stopped and asked the usual annoying questions about Serena's jewelry— was it real silver, what kinds of stones were they— but she was no longer interested. Daniel had made something new that none of the other vendors had. That was infinitely more interesting than pencil tops and would bring a higher price. Walking back uptown made their feet ache, but the weather was humid, and they could barely tolerate the subway anyway. Daniel had saved all the drawings he'd been working on: pieces of London, Tokyo, Paris, with pretty miniatures of Reims and Notre Dame, an entire relief map of China with the Great Wall across it, and Australia, with the port city of Sidney clearly visible and painted turquoise, the Great Barrier Reef. "When?" she asked, amazed, looking at a miniature United States where the Golden Gate Bridge rose out of one edge like a folding cardboard puzzle.

"When did you have time to do this?"

"When you were sewing, see? I went to the library," confessed Daniel.

Selling globes in the Village and in Soho took on its own enchanted rhythm. Serena knew when the crowds changed, where the money was, where the pleasant conversations could be expected. Sometimes there were cappuccinos offered by artists, people who considered Daniel and Serena artists as well and insisted on talking in cafes. Daniel watched, bemused, while these new friends spent the price of an entire meal on a cup of coffee on Bleecker Street. Serena seldom had anything to say, but she enjoyed meeting these women who held hands with other women, who liked Daniel's work, but didn't fawn all over him like schoolgirls. The men were more chummy, Argentinians, Brazilians, Japanese from San Francisco. Daniel and Serena gossiped to each other about who was seeing whom among the Village crowd. The possibilities were endless.

Until Tiger arrived on the scene. It was a brisk day, sunny and dry, and Serena sat cross legged on an orange cushion in Washington Square Park. Her jewels and the globes were placed neatly on a suitcase with wooden legs that she had rigged up. She was filled with a sense of well being, and she closed her eyes, braiding her glossy black hair, absorbing the sunlight. Sitting on a park bench, Daniel played chess with Doreen, a woman with playful eyes, one of the cappuccino drinkers whom Serena had decided to seduce. Or more accurately, to be seduced by her. It was just a matter of time.

With her eyes closed, she sensed Daniel stopping in the middle of the game. A young, striking woman had stopped in

57

front of them. She was pale, dressed in black, except for tiger-striped tights, a little torn at the knee. Her hair was dyed black, and blond roots incongruously rose out of her round head. But she had marvelous golden eyes which Daniel fixed on immediately, and Serena felt her stomach shrink with anxiety.

"My name is Tiger," she said, breathlessly, extending a beringed, though slightly dirty, hand to Daniel. Doreen instinctively closed ranks with Serena, their collective brownness attempting to shield each other from Tiger's deathly pallor.

The afternoon had suddenly changed. All that seemed right before her was now teetering in the balance. Serena watched her brother turn into a beast before her eyes, tuning his spirit in synch with this newcomer and leaving her behind as if she were the younger sibling. He spoke with Tiger as if he'd always known English, not stumbling or looking to Serena for help. Inside, Serena found herself leaping from one contingency plan to another. She was again the desperate sister begging the orphanage in Guayaquil not to separate Daniel from her, feeling betrayed and not knowing on which account she felt the most hurt. Was it that Daniel had chosen this bizarre American, or that he suddenly asserted his macho privilege and demanded his due?

As evening mellowed the sounds of the City, the four drifted towards the cafes and the kindred wanderers out for a night of bohemian adventure. Tiger maintained Daniel on her wavelength, praising his work and, unluckily for Serena, disclosing proudly that she was also an artist. It wasn't quite dark when, momentarily diverted by Doreen's embrace, Serena noticed that her brother and Tiger had left their group. She searched the faces of her companions, blond and dark, bearded and smooth, sober and intoxicated, trying to determine when they'd slipped away. In Doreen's face, she met her own concern, but no one seemed to grasp her situation. Behind her chair, she found the suitcase still there, but in her bag there was less than half the money they'd made that day, and the key to their room, dangling from a leather thong tied to her piece of amber, was also gone.

"He lied to me, Doreen," she sobbed into Doreen's waiting arms, who assumed Serena was talking about her brother. But Serena was thinking about Amin, who had told her she could do things with the amber, and now it was gone. Her room was gone, her life was gone. Daniel was going to be just like the other men in Guayaquil, fat, drunk, with a wife to support and screaming, dirty little kids to feed.

Doreen had three roommates back at her apartment on Ludlow Street. Serena marveled at their faces, so different from one another, yet motivated by something familiar. They took her in and fed her, clothed her, and mostly left her alone to enjoy Doreen's company. She did enjoy Doreen. With beguiling eyes, she seemed to drink her in with all her stories, laughter, passionate kisses, and the golden time that stretched before them like a tapestry of pleasure. Serena had to remind herself that she was miserable, that she had no home, no job, no brother, that she should be crying, not uttering songs of ecstasy, but it was impossible to remember her problems for long. "You can stay here," assured Doreen, lips pursed in a kiss, "we can make beautiful jewelry together."

Four days later, Daniel showed up at her stand near Lincoln Center, his face thinner, his clothes wrinkled and a little musty. Doreen took a walk to let Serena speak with him, but Daniel didn't have much to say. He showed her his neck, covered with reddish love marks, his eyes tired and regaining their usual indolence, and handed her the amber with the key back.

"She's gone," he told his sister. "Tiger insisted this piece of amber was making her sick, so she left." Serena rubbed the amber between her fingers, thinking, but not really thinking. Daniel took up his pencil and began to sketch again, pyramids and the Nile, the Sphinx, the contour of North Africa, the biggest map she had seen him draw. After a while, Serena looked up and saw Doreen, strolling among the tourists, sharing an ice cream cone with another girl.

At night, Daniel slept soundly while Serena stayed awake, stroking the amber, looking at the full moon through their dusty windows, planning a future with Daniel, perhaps even with Doreen. From her window she could catch a glimpse of the other moon, the one on the weird fountain that had attracted her brother's attention that night, next to the Cathedral, and had started him off on drawing the globes. He was a funny kid, though he wasn't a kid any longer. One day there would be a woman who would take him away, who would make him forget the years in the orphanage, their journey to a new land, but that was life. And she had always known that someday she, too, would search for her own happiness, not just money, or a home. But for the moment, it was too soon to dream.

৯৯

When we cleared the tea things away, dusted off the bread crumbs, and put away the tablecloths, the metal surface of the tables became our desks and it was time to study. Or, to plan revenge. Mirella and I were best friends, sworn to the death and sealed in blood with Sister Prudencia's kitchen knife. My cut got infected. But Mirella, who was very butch, rugged, volatile, green-eyed Mirella with the black braids, and me, ready for anything, still were no match for the older girls in the dorm next to us.

The girls from the second dorm had ambushed us the week before, and Mirella and I had paid dearly for that. They waited until we were washed and had on clean socks, all ready for breakfast on a Monday morning, and they jumped us. Magda let out a yell to warn us, but it was too late because the entire second dorm was on top of us, painting streaks on our faces with the ink markers, on our shirt collar, on our ears, necks, backs of our hands, even Mirella's shins when she kicked as hard as she could. The nuns came in and stopped the fight, terror painted on their faces; ours were smeared in black and red.

61

There were punishments, of course. The first and second dorms got prayer every morning from six to seven and at night from ten to ten thirty; they didn't want to keep us up too late. The third dorm where the little girls slept got to help sister Prudencia in the kitchen for a week, for not telling what they knew.

The intrigue was going back to the beginning of the year; first the night when Mirella and I short-sheeted all the beds in the second dorm while Magda played lookout, then the night when they tied up our wet socks so tight we couldn't get dressed in the morning. We had to cut off the tops and wear them like that. Then, Magda came up with the bright idea.

We would tell them, through the grapevine of course, that Mirella was sick, so sick that she had only one month to live. It was easy. The first day of our lie, Mirella got her period and she was so pale with cramps and nausea that sister Rebeca sent her to the dorm from Math class. Our enemies were visibly shaken. Magda and I were smug. I got to bring Mirella her dinner in bed for three days.

This was not what made the girls in the second dorm so mad, but the fact that when a month went by Mirella still had not died, and several of them had given her presents. And we had become very close, with Mirella sharing everything with me: candy, gum, and the Beatles 45 which we could only look at, since we had nowhere to play it. For a dying girl, Mirella was surprisingly healthy, and the two of us with Magda appeared to be quite happy awaiting death.

This was why our classmates in the other dorm had it in for us so bad that they decided to paint us with the markers. The ink took a week to wash off and our dorm hated us for making them pray so much. And then, the new girl came to our school in the foothills of Antofagasta.

The first day Susana showed up at recess, it was clear that she was someone special. She stood out. We could point her out from a crowd of thirteen year old girls all wearing the same uniform. She was different from the rest of us.

Mirella wrinkled her nose and shoved me, hoping I would stop staring at the new comer and go run around the school yard with her instead. Or maybe go hide behind the swings and smoke a cigarette. I was glued to the ground. Magdalena said the new girl had money. It showed in her store-bought navy blue uniform, not home made like ours. Magda knew about the quality of cloth and such things, so I trusted her appraisal.

When the nuns escorted Susana to the dorms, Sister Reyes rang the bell signaling the end of our recess period. All four hundred girls lined up by the corridor in descending order from 12th to 1st grade, and in ascending order by height. All of us short girls in the eight grade lined up at the front of our class with practiced movements, representing the current order of best friendships, rivalries, platonic betrothals, and eternally sworn vendettas. We walked up the stairs to our Spanish grammar class, carefully clicking and dragging the heels of our shoes, which was the latest fashion for any girl who considered herself "in the know."

Sister Tomasa, meanwhile, would have none of our buzzing and calculated dawdling, and insisted we sit down at once with our hands folded on our laps. After a brief benediction, she adjusted the wire-rim specs on her plump face and opened the formidable *Gramática de la Academia Real Española* upon her desk. It was going to be a long afternoon.

Sitting at the front of the class, Susana was not only pretty, she looked better than everybody else. Her glossy brown hair in a "pageboy" looked right out of a European magazine, her shirts were starched, her hands bore no ink stains. She looked clean, but she didn't look clean-cut. The girl was hip. She had a round face the color of nutmeg, with a small nose and freckles, always-red lips curved in a smile that one could only call mischievous. She wore tortoise shell rimmed glasses that made her brown eyes more penetrating, and she spoke with a lilt in her voice that denoted just the right amount of disdain for authority.

The dorms were divided into single rooms for the seniors and three large common rooms for about 70 boarding students. The large rooms were supervised by a stark cubicle where a nun slept. I knew the cubicles were stark because one night, before Mirella and I had become friends, she threw my shoes over the dividing screen and I had no choice but to break in and retrieve them. The single rooms were mostly reserved for the 12th graders and the students known as having "a delicate constitution." The rest of us shared the large rooms, cold floors, and lumpy mattresses, but mostly, we had the time of our lives. The nuns, guided by some unfathomable motive, assigned Susana to the dorm with the fourth graders. I never even got to see her brush her teeth.

An interesting thing about Susana, and a measure of her hipness, was that she always seemed to be where the action was. Although she was taller than the group I ran with by about two inches, there was no question that she would join us. She was the only girl who actually stole cigarettes from a visiting priest, when we dared her. She was the one caught giggling when the volley ball hit Sister Tomasa on the head. And although I was sick at the time, I was told that Susana was the one who volunteered to go wipe the floor when Pilar threw up in study hall. As the school year unfolded and the eighth grade struggled through its collective puberty, all of my waking fantasies centered around kissing Susana.

There were the times in study hall when, sitting quietly across from Susana at the end of the long table, I felt I could kiss her quickly, watch her brown eyes widen, then return to my notebook. Sister Rebeca would be completely absorbed by her math book, the meager lighting from the bare yellowish light bulbs bringing Susana's round cheek into golden relief, and somehow very close to my own face. Other times I would imagine Susana dropping her veil in church while kneeling next to me, and through a series of complicated maneuvers she would kiss me hard on the lips, causing me to stifle a gasp rather than betray my pleasure. The best fantasy was probably the one where she would faint on Sunday from the frankincense in church, and Sister Rebeca would order me to loosen the navy blue ribbon around her shirt collar and wet her brow and her neck with holy water. Of course the holy water business was highly unlikely and probably sacrilegious, but the scenario required that Susana would faint behind the confessional so I could help her regain consciousness with soft kisses, then deeper kisses, while moistening her neck, as Sister had instructed.

With all this fantasizing came a different way of looking at myself. I had to fit into the roles I was imagining, so I developed a glib, chatty personality. I delivered smart-aleck monologues in class, one-liners in recess, gossip and innuendo in the dorms, and soon charmed Susana into being my new best friend. I became devilishly calculating, hoping to seize the opportunity of this all important kiss. I came to understand that the situations I easily dreamed up were far more difficult to engineer in real life. The chance encounters near the shower, the accidental touch of her hand while cleaning the erasers, the arm carelessly draped over Susana's shoulder during gym class and even getting her as a partner in French class while we conjugated together, rolled our r's and pursed our lips— these took constant planning, so I practiced.

But I practiced with the wrong girl. My new personality also had an effect on the girl with whom I had sworn undying allegiance and who still had the nick on her finger to prove it. Mirella had no problem pinning me to the chalkboard, only to stare intently into my eyes, then walking away leaving me breathless. Mirella's hand was the one to brush mine when I dropped *my* veil in church, making me blush while her eyes drank me in. It was Mirella who saved me from falling off the ladder when we were stealing grapes in the garden, and she the one to suck the splinter off my pinky.

Spring arrived, and although one could hardly tell the difference in our desert town, we knew because the water in the pitchers was not so cold in the mornings. We rose at six and went directly to get a pitcher of water to pour into the basins. We stood all in a row, feet balancing sideways on the cold tile, pink and white nightgowns making little children of pretentious adolescents. Braids and pony tails pinned up, we scrubbed our sleepy faces to the sound of chattering teeth, roosters crowing, mocking birds, and the bells of the chapel.

It was during music class that Sister Margarita took up the weekly ritual of having us practice our Ave Verum in the Park. She could barely open the gates before we would rush out like frenzied pigeons into the street. Once in the park, we would wander through the lanes singing and harmonizing, possessed of a fervor that was hardly religious. Susana, Mirella, Magda and I had by then become inseparable, linking arms and trailing proudly behind Sister Margarita, our spiritual leader.

As for my fantasies, they didn't exist for me in this exalted state. I never saw it coming, then, when Susana leaned against a tree and Magda placed on her lips that perfect kiss I had been planning. They stood there, holding hands, Magda removing her own eyeglasses to kiss Susana again, while I was twirling faster and faster into a dead faint.

I came to rather quickly. Mirella's lips were very hot against mine. She was flawless in her technique causing wild palpitations in my breast. For a brief moment, I was confused, but only for a moment. Sister Margarita was coming around the bend and I had no time to linger on this first lesson in romance, only to kiss Mirella back, while Susana was still looking.

&

Original in Spanish
"Gabriela"
Compañeras: Latina Lesbians

That amazing summer of my fifteenth year shines like the very sun in my memory, yet it is a hidden episode that would send my friends reeling if they knew. During that time, my father's small hardware store in the commercial district of Concepción was in financial crisis. My mother, who taught grammar at the Liceo #6, was planning to work with him over the summer to recover the deficit in the family business.

"We can't leave the girl alone," Mamá said at tea time. In our small Colonial house situated in the old part of Concepción, the afternoon sun filtered through the street fence, and the flies buzzed and stuck to the lace curtain, now somewhat yellowed with age.

"Have her come to work at the store with us," said Papá, stirring his tea. "She should make herself useful, that girl." Papá was convinced that making oneself useful was the solution to everything. Mamá guided the plate with toast toward him.

"The city just isn't a place for a young lady in the summer," she said observing the windows. "All the trade school boys will stick to her like flies. We'd better send her to the country."

"Isn't there any marmalade left?" I asked in the hope of being included.

I arrived in the country wearing a flowered sundress, sandals, and white knee socks, my hair in a ponytail tied with a white ribbon. I looked just as lost there as the folks who arrive from San Fernando to sell flowers in Santiago. My aunts thought it was wonderful to have their well-behaved niece staying with them for the summer. The three of them hugged and kissed me until I thought I would suffocate. My arrival, meanwhile, had not gone unnoticed by the other farmers. They had gathered by the gate to greet me. Compared to my pale city complexion, theirs looked tan and healthy. My younger aunts, Hortensia and Violeta, introduced me while tía Elvira went back into the house.

Among the people who shared the land, women and young girls, and some men, there was a boy in a white shirt, dark, wearing a large chupaya that shadowed his eyes. He stared at me, seemingly amused, and hid behind his family.

The summers Mamá and I had spent with my three maiden aunts were a childhood pleasure well-remembered. The house was light and smelled fresh, painted white, without curtains or tapestries, or embroidered doilies.

On the wall hung one or two of tía Elvira's watercolors and bunches of dried herbs tied with bright ribbon. Tía Elvira was the only one who read and did so assiduously. Hortensia and Violeta preferred to make pine wood furniture in their shop behind the house. The two of them were excellent carpenters, and all three subsisted in winter from the sale of Hortensia and Violeta's finely crafted pieces.

I ran to my little room next to the shop where they had placed flowers in a Coca-Cola bottle and a pine frame mirror on the night stand. I yanked the white ribbon from my hair and sat on the bed pulling off my sandals and knee socks. I felt better that way. I was anxious to go out in the sun, to run through the wheat field stirring up the little yellow butterflies. Besides, it was also important to show that I wasn't just any stuck-up kid from the city.

Outside, the country offered me the delights I remembered. I would go to the river or wander around in the fields, happily smiling at the sun. I gathered tiny forget-me-nots and daisies, and placed them in a vase on the kitchen table. My aunts worked in the vegetable gardens and the other people attended to their work in their fields. Sometimes they would ask for help, but it was only to entertain me. Mostly, they let me do whatever I wished.

After three or four days, I was getting some color in my cheeks and on my arms. Freckles appeared on my nose as usual. One morning, I got up as soon as I awoke and went to the shop while braiding my hair because I had heard voices. The boy with the chupaya was there, talking with tía Violeta!

"There you are, niece," she said. "Go with Gabriel and get fresh eggs." So saying, tía Violeta handed me a basket and ushered us outside. The boy looked at me out of the corner of his eye, and taking my hand, he ran with me toward the chicken coops. Through feathers flying and sonorous cackling, I looked at him suspiciously. I didn't find boys very amusing. Realizing I was watching him, he smiled and said: "What happened? Did your stockings get dirty?" He laughed, and I was surprised at how clear his laughter seemed. The poor hens were furious with my clumsy movements; it was no easy task to scoop the eggs out of their nests without disturbing them.

In the kitchen, my three aunts had breakfast well under way and I gave the basket to tía Hortensia.

"Sit down, girls," she said, and I turned with a gasp to look at Gabriel who had taken off the chupaya.

The shiny black hair, very short and straight like a boy's, was undoubtedly that of a fifteen-year-old girl. Gabriela, then it's Gabriela, I thought, blushing to the tips of my fingernails while Gabriela, smiling, watched me, her teeth white as pearls, and deep set black eyes shaded by long, straight lashes.

I don't know if anyone noticed, but I was sure that there was steam coming out of my ears, I felt so feverish. Gabriela chatted amiably with my aunts, shaking her shiny hair from time to time, looking at me with a smile that literally made my knees tremble. Although I barely touched the food, I felt as if I had eaten an ox. The only thing I could think about was running outside again, holding Gabriela's hand. After breakfast, she had to go work with her family. I went to the river and lay on the grass. Through the bayberry bushes blooming like suns in the wind, I could see the figure of Gabriela bending over in the field. Once, she pushed her hat back and wiped her forehead with her sleeve. Not knowing why, I was overtaken by an irrepressible sadness and cried in silence, listening to the water splashing against the rocks and the whisper of the willows in the summer breeze.

"Tía, tía! I need a chupaya!" I said as I went running into the shop to see tía Violeta and almost slipped on the sawdust that covered the floor.

"Careful, you'll get a sliver in your foot, Tina," warned my aunt while she sawed off a board.

"I won't, tía, because I almost have callouses now, like Gabriela," I began.

"Oh, well. If it's callouses you want," she said turning back to her work. "But why don't you wear your pretty straw hat with the cherries?"

"But we're going horseback riding by the Springs, and the girls will tease me," I explained gravely. In my mind I could already see myself mortified by the amused looks of Gabriela and her cousin. My aunt lent me an old chupaya that was even a little moth-eaten on the edge, and I went happily out to meet my friends.

Gabriela was waiting for me by the gate with her cousin Elena, who had a freckled face and green eyes. That's why she was called "la Rucia."

Our three horses were bayos with woolen mantas to avoid getting their sweat on our legs; mine had a daisy behind her ear. I stepped on a large clay pot and scrambled to mount. Gabriela watched me while she rolled a straw reed between lips and tongue.

"Hold on tight to her mane," la Rucia reminded me.

"Yes, I know."

We began to ride toward the river, my heart beating hard. Gabriela was very quiet.

"What's up?" I asked.

"It's just that Manuel thinks he hit it off with you," said la Rucia. I made a horrible face and she laughed.

"Seriously, Tina," said Gabriela, "remember when Manuel told my mother that he had to come along to take care of us?"

"But that doesn't mean anything!" said la Rucia, winking at me.

"Chito said that Manuel was going to *court* you," Gabriela confronted me, held onto the mane of my horse, leaned over until our hats touched. "So, don't start flirting with Manuel, okay?"

"I promise," I said, happy that she cared so much about me. La Rucia gave Gabriela a shove and teased her.

"Gabriela is scared of guys. Not me. Let a prince come and get me!" La Rucia shook her long hair and raised her face to the sun, proud of her looks. Gabriela slapped la Rucia's horse and clicked her tongue, sending the animal downhill at a hard gallop while la Rucia screamed and swore at us. Gabriela and I rode behind her, yelling: "Careful, *Princesa!*"

As we turned by the oaks, we met face to face with Manuel and Chito, who had stopped la Rucia's horse. She took full advantage of the situation to impress Chito.

"You almost made me fall down that hill!" said la Rucia to Gabriela in a breathless voice.

"That's a lie!" Gabriela was arrogant and sat straight on her horse like her brother Manuel. I was proud of her.

"Good day, Chito, Manuel," I said, to appease matters. The boys tipped their hats way back in greeting. To tease them, I took off my hat and bowed, which made everyone laugh. La Rucia pretended to be hot and steered her horse to the shade of an oak covered with red copihues. Chito looked at her wistfully, she looked so striking with her long hair against the red flowers.

"Chito," said Manuel, giving him a knowing look.

"I won't be joining you today," said Chito, a bit resentful.

"What a pity!" la Rucia threw him a kiss and the boy waved goodbye riding uphill. Manuel, handsome like Gabriela, offered to get me a set of reins, leaning attentively toward me.

"No, thanks. I'm an amazon," I said, solemn, and galloped behind Gabriela who deserved the title more than I.

The day was beautiful. Though it was very hot, I doubt I noticed it because I always felt a little feverish next to Gabriela. Our ride to the Springs was at times a tense game between

Gabriela and Manuel, with me as the coveted damsel. When he flanked my right, she cut between us and rode easily beside me. Manuel pretended not to notice and chatted with la Rucia.

When we arrived at the Springs, we dismounted and tied the horses in the shade. From the high rocks, a thousand sprays of crystalline water fell to the river. We were in the loveliest part of the river's journey, where it opened and strayed among the rocks, forming little pools of water, cold as snow.

"This water comes directly from the Andes," Manuel sought to explain.

"You don't say, *professor*," said Gabriela.

"They say you can find precious stones here," continued Manuel, ignoring the comment, and placing some pebbles in my hand.

"Why don't you make her a necklace, then," interrupted Gabriela. I burst out laughing, hugging her with pleasure. La Rucia also laughed, and Manuel could not stand it anymore.

"If you're going to behave like this, I'm leaving!" he warned. The three of us linked arms and danced in the shallow water, chanting:

"Emeralds and rubies, viva! viva! We have jewels!"

"The devil take you, crazy women!" said Manuel menacingly as he picked up his canteen and mounted his horse without looking at us. We kept dancing and singing until we saw him disappear through the willows.

La Rucia took off her blouse and lay down in the sun, still laughing at the unfortunate Manuel. I tried to braid my hair again, but it was all tangled. Gabriela took an elastic from her pocket and quickly tied it in a knot for me without saying a word. The coolness I felt on my neck was delicious and I looked at her

gratefully. She also looked at me, with those dreamy eyes and that irresistible smile. Suddenly, I felt dizzy.

"Let's go swimming," I urged, pulling off my shirt. Gabriela followed me to the water, but when she took off her blouse, I almost fainted. Gabriela wasn't skinny like me. She already had round breasts and a shapely waist. I dove in the cold water to hide my anxiety and opened my eyes to see as Gabriela swam easily in the strong current, and it was hard to follow her.

Soon, Elena joined us, and we searched for little red pebbles, playing at being mermaids. La Rucia did look like a mermaid, with her light hair and green pants.

"Hey, what are *amazons*?" asked Gabriela between dives.

"They were ancient warriors. In Greece or Africa, I think. They were excellent riders, and they didn't like men," I told them.

"Really?" La Rucia was surprised.

"Really. They had spears and swords, and they would go to war. They were very brave." I was pleased with myself, being able to offer such an interesting tale. My friends listened attentively. I embroidered on the details of Amazon life.

When we got cold in the water, we lay in the sun. Gabriela and I looked at each other, she with half-closed lids shading the sun, while droplets fell from her black lashes to her red lips. I felt like crying. On the way home, we stopped at every blackberry bush and devoured all but the last berry, staining our lips and our fingers purple. La Rucia got stung by a bee and started to cry. Gabriela hugged her cousin, but she also told her that Amazons didn't cry. I agreed. When we arrived, tía Hortensia met us, a little concerned. Manuel had told her that we had gotten lost.

"I'll kill him," said la Rucia. "I never get lost."

"That's true, dear. Well, the food is ready," said my aunt.

Tía Elvira came out to the back yard, under the arbor where the summer table was set, and she placed pastel de choclo next to the stone where the hot peppers were ground.

"Do you like ají?" asked Gabriela.

"No, it's too spicy," I told her.

"But it's good, look." She ran her finger over the stone, then licked it. I stared at her to see if she screamed because it was so hot, but she licked her lips with pleasure.

"See?" she smiled, and it was then that Gabriela came close to me and gave me a kiss on the lips, so soft, that I kissed her back because I wanted more of that softness, and of the spicy taste of ají.

Towards the end of January, there was a drought and it got terribly hot. We all worked hard to water the fields and the gardens at dawn, before the sun could burn the plants. In the evenings, my aunts sat with the ladies, and I would go for a short ride with la Rucia and Gabriela. La Rucia liked to be Queen of the Amazons, while Gabriela and I were her generals. We would ride in the open field until we arrived at our favorite hill, and when the sun blazed over the horizon in the early evening, I remembered that in March I would have to go back to school and leave my companions.

"Amazons were not sentimental," Gabriela said to me one evening, noticing my silence, but I could not have explained the confusion I felt. We sat among the poppies, and la Rucia sang some ballads. Gabriela listened quietly, with her eternal blade of grass between her lips, and then the three of us sang a song by Violeta Parra.

On Sundays, the families in the area gathered at dusk under a large arbor where there was a parrillada. Later, we would dance cuecas and refalosas with renewed energy in the cool night air.

When night fell, the guitars were tuned and the party began, Manuel always proud to be playing with the older men. Gabriela's mother plaintively suggested we put on dresses to dance the cueca, but la Rucia told her that warriors didn't wear dresses. Chito played a harp that had been left to him by his grandfather, and la Rucia sang with her sister, Raquel. In the midst of such happiness, it was hard to grasp what I felt. Sometimes, Gabriela would take my hand, and together we watched the couples dancing. At times, we would dance with all the little girls and boys and with la Rucia, while Chito devoted his most anguished looks to her.

The last night in January, I didn't want to sing or dance. I slipped away to be home alone in my inexplicable melancholy. Around midnight, my aunts returned, hot and tired, but happy.

"Violeta, look at our niece, sitting here alone," said tía Elvira.

"Are you sad, dear?" asked tía Violeta.

"No, tía."

"She must miss her parents."

"No, tía. It's just that I want to think. May I sleep out here on the hammock?"

My aunts exchanged a look and smiled. "As you like, dear," said tía Hortensia. "But take a blanket so you don't get chilled."

My three aunts kissed me like fairy godmothers, blessing my sleep. I remained, staring at the moon, thinking that perhaps Gabriela could come to Concepción with tía Elvira in the winter. Soon, I gave in to sleep and dozed off, leaning on the post by the hammock.

"How much chicha did you drink?" whispered Gabriela in my ear.

"Gabriela!" I was startled out of my dream. "What time is it?"

"Who knows. Nighttime," she said. "Did you get kicked out?"

"No, it's too hot. And you?"

"Me too; I can't sleep. Why did you leave?"

Since I did not know how to answer, I stared at my feet. They were tanned, and the hair on my legs seemed lightened by the sun. Next to mine, Gabriela's legs were much stronger. For her, the work at the farm was not merely a summertime diversion. It was her life.

"We're growing, do you realize?" I said, finally.

"What else? Everyone grows," Gabriela sat on the hammock, swinging her legs.

"But, what will you do,?" I sat on the hammock with her, wanting to ask a million questions. "Will you get married?"

"Who, me? Never!" she said vehemently.

"Really?"

"Sure. Now, I'm an Amazon."

"Seriously, Gabriela," I said.

"Seriously. Let's go to the poppies. Want to?"

"Now?" I looked at the full moon. Gabriela jumped down from the hammock and gave me her hand. I jumped, and we went running without stopping until we arrived at the hill, plush with poppies, from where we could see the houses and the glow of the remaining embers under the large arbor. We lay among the flowers, listening to the crickets and the bark of a dog now and then. After a long time, I turned my head to tell Gabriela that I was sleepy and saw her asleep. She was so beautiful that I leaned closer to look at her, her long lashes, her smooth forehead, her lips delicately drawn. When she opened her eyes, I kissed her quickly, afraid she would move away. Gabriela sighed and wrapped her arms around my neck.

"One more, give me another kiss," she said in my ear. Then there was no moon, there were no poppies, only Gabriela with her shiny hair in my hands, her warm breath, the weight of her firm legs, and the beating of my heart against hers.

Near dawn, I dipped my mouth to her breast, reaching with my tongue for the circle on her nipples that made her sigh and moan, that deep sound that rose from her mouth, red and swollen, as she kissed me again and again until I forgot everything and remembered everything: from the first day I saw her and thought she was a boy to the moment when I knew she was a girl, when I saw her golden, swimming in the river, so strong and beautiful. How was it possible that she would let me kiss her dear breasts, that sweet waist, and raise her belly just curving to meet my mouth?

Morning arrived pink with the singing of the birds, the buzzing of the bees, and my own sighs while Gabriela parted my legs and I grasped her hand, her mouth searching the wetness and the warmth that flowed from me. Around me, there were the flowers and the wind, a murmur and a silence. I trembled in her hands, her tongue more urgent each time, until there was nothing more than the blue sky and all my being transformed by a new feeling, a sigh, something sweet, deep, immense, Gabriela.

Since the night of the poppies, Gabriela and I spent the month of February submerged in our delight, not caring about anything else. I had gotten almost as dark as she from being in the sun and swimming nude in the river. In the afternoons, we would stay with my aunts, seated in the shade of the arbor, eating watermelon and listening to tía Elvira who enjoyed reading poetry, but towards the end of the month, my joy ceased abruptly with Mamá's arrival from Concepción to visit my aunts, her older sisters. When she saw that I was so tanned, barefoot, with my hair unbraided, Mamá was scandalized and decided to take me immediately back to *civilization*.

The train to Concepción ran along the vineyards, and from far off one could see the bunches of grapes, purple, green, or pink. Thinking constantly about Gabriela, I leaned my head on the dusty window of the train, letting tears roll down my face, while Mamá talked with the lady from Licantén. I wiped my face quickly each time they asked me something.

"Where does your daughter go to school?" asked the lady.

"Answer, girl" said Mamá.

"The Liceo #3 with the Spanish nuns," I mumbled.

"They are *sisters*, Tina. It's vulgar to call them 'nuns'," chided Mamá.

"Don't say it, then," was my insolent retort, because I cared little by that time.

"Please excuse her, Señora," said Mamá poking my ribs. "She has become completely wild in the country." The lady nodded at everything. I was grateful that at least they weren't watching me.

"She didn't even wear sandals. She has callouses on her feet!" Mamá confided to the lady aboard the train.

"Ave María!" exclaimed the pious woman.

The last Sunday we spent together, Gabriela and I escaped to the Springs on horseback. The sun was high and we took refuge under a willow with our feet in the water. Looking at Gabriela, I realized she had grown more than I had. She had ripened like the taut grapes we gathered for the fresh chicha.

"Gabriela, you're so beautiful, I want to die!" I said, kissing her cheek.

"Don't be a fool," she kissed me back.

"For you I'm a fool," I insisted. She lowered her gaze and I suffered untold miseries while her long lashes shaded her pretty face. Her hair had grown, and it curled in soft waves around her neck.

"Tina, look at me," she demanded. I looked at her and we held hands.

"Do you realize that we're really Amazons, you and I? La Rucia isn't anymore, since she went with Chito." She looked very seriously at me.

"That's true," I said

"Then, promise."

"What should I promise?" I asked.

"That you'll come back here when you're free," she said simply.

"I promise. Gabriela, I promise with all my heart!"

Between sobs and the already distant sensation of her red lips, I was shaken by Mamá's hand and the train racing by at dusk.

"Why do you cry, my girl? You've fallen asleep," she said.

"I promise, I promise," I blurted out, still wanting to hold on to Gabriela in my reverie.

"Ay, Virgen! What's wrong with her?" pleaded Mamá.

"She has sun stroke," offered the lady from Licantén. "You have to give her a very strong tea . . ."

"No, no! Give me chicha fresca!" I said, stupidly.

"Tina!" Mamá was horrified. "Ave María, it must have been those country boys. As soon as we return, I'll send you to boarding school with the 'nuns' and not a word out of you!" came the verdict.

81

"Sí, Mamita," I said, closing my eyes and smiling to the memory of Gabriela.

≥

chupaya: wide-brimmed straw hat
bayos: yellowish brown horses
mantas: blankets
la Rucia: "Blondie"
copihues: the flower of Chile that grows like a vine and looks like an upside down tulip; they can be red, white, or pink
pastel de choclo: a traditional dish of meat and corn
ají: hot pepper
parrillada: open air roast for a large number of people
cuecas and refalosas: typical Southern Chilean dances
chicha: hard grape cider that is very sweet and intoxicating

I. Late to Work

Boston wakes me late one Spring morning, rising heavy and gray over wet streets. I close the window, wipe the rain from the sill, then the sleep from my brain with a hand through my hair. I blink to focus the shape of lamp posts or trees in the fog.

My bed appears passive and cold, and I am not tempted to linger. The tussle of images persists behind fading dreams that cannot be exorcised with water or toothpaste.

Raincoats are always cold, willing accomplices to bad weather in April; mine dangles in tormenting reminder from its hook; it may be weeks before the sun. On the porch, the sweet smell of new leaves surrounds me. I pause to see the buds on the old tree; its branches shake in the wind and splatter me with cold rain.

Because of a gnawing little animal hiding in my stomach, I go into the doughnut shop to join other embittered souls peering into their coffee. Hearing a little Spanish being spoken, I feel comforted enough to seek a swivel chair on which to sulk away the rest of the time I've stolen from work this morning. A loudspeaker transmits scratchy versions of Boy George and Roberta Flack, but the gritty team of blue-suited officers hears nothing. They cackle rhythmically, heaving sinister strains of laughter, while their CB's sputter cop lingo to each other.

Behind the counter, stand young Dorchester amazons possessed of a quick tongue. Ignoring their customers they discuss their inscrutable boyfriends in a wide, flat inflection rising above the cop static, the smoke, the Latin gossip, the glint of a regulation revolver being caressed by a fat, pink hand. These girls are not intimidated. "Can't cha smile," says the cop. "Dollah even," says the girl, extending her hand. Next to me, the conversation turns contemplative. "No la has visto?" dice uno. "Se aburrió de mi," le contesta el otro con pena.

It's after ten. I imagine an office full of anxious talk: "Is she sick/pregnant/boyfriend trouble? Doesn't shave her legs, does she?" I imagine the route I must follow to reach that sterile place, the holes on Mass Ave, the stretch of construction lined by raincoated burlies making more holes in the street. If the sun were shining, they would be exposing sweat on hairy chests, grunting their hormonal excess at unwilling, scurrying beings on heels.

Waiting for the light at Comm Ave, I'll greet the first magnolia tree that bloomed this year, its darling blossoms bewildered by the acid rain and exhaust fumes, yet, beautiful, bewitching against that old pink building with the green, rusted copper moldings. I am so happy to see the magnolia, the dogwood, the forsythia speckling sun on the sidewalk! Why drive obediently to a murderous office reeking of hierarchy and engagement rings?

When my fem-mobile reaches the river, shock absorbers screaming from the workout, the Beacon Street light will undoubtedly turn red. I'll position myself on the left lane without signaling, so as to get the advantage of jumping out unexpectedly to make a left turn. It's the only way to beat the caravan of hefty trucks and exec-mobiles crossing the bridge. Owing to this habit I have of digressing famously at intersections, I'll miss the jump on the wheeling mob and will meekly await a break in the traffic or a waving hand to make my turn. Sliding onto Storrow Drive I'll bounce over the last few holes and patches of tar to race along the river, finally unencumbered by traffic lights. Time to turn up the radio and hum, hum, harmonize.

Another sea gull crossing the river stirs a breeze in my heart, the softest light across the water, the unexplainable delight in watching the river and the bridges in any weather, dark or dawn, singing *"you're the one, you're the one who took my soul,"* and then I've lost the motivation to sulk any longer. Willows, tender and yellow wave me by; a regatta stuffed with naive freshmen rows by in the rain. A gentle cloud uncovers a patch of sky, and perhaps I won't work late tonight. Perhaps I'll make a long distance call and charge it to the office, and place her photograph on my desk and stare at her face with adoring eyes. Perhaps I've never been in love like this. It's Spring. It makes me feverish.

II. Daylight

Daylight changed without you. The weather got colder; it rained, the sun came out, wet newspapers dried on the street corner, pigeons fluttered about the park, children squealed on the sidewalk wearing witch faces and pumpkin heads, half-eaten candy apples melted on their sleeves . . .

Another day went by. Your side of the bed got rumpled, too, I borrowed your pillow, whispered your name, opened the window and blew at the dust, tilted the lamp shade, breathed in the twilight . . .

I noticed the sounds of leaves rustling, of trains approaching underground, of women laughing a little like you. I conjured up your face and traced your lips in the air, thinking, your absence is different now. There's no anxiety, only discomfort, a stillness about everything— time doesn't move the same way. My thoughts are quieter.

I thought I'd get more work done without you, I was wrong. I got the mail and paid the bills, flipped the calendar to November, munched on the yellow quince I bought because it smelled like my childhood, but it had no flavor . . .

The weather changed again. The night is restless with warm wind and radios blaring, the sound of car horns bending at the corner. Before I sleep, there will be hollow moments of missing you. I know you'll be here tomorrow . . . what frightens me is knowing this is how it would be if you were really gone, leaving my skin slowly, carving out the time, until I finally feel your absence surrounding me like mist, taking shape, like the depth of your eyes and the scent of your body.

ತಿ

at *government center* i sat down exhausted and stared at the tracks. i was sad. sad, because there were indentations along the subway cave and i knew what they were for.

i imagined myself, caught along the cave somewhere, running, inhaling the dusty air, breathing all that air full of dirt and soot, and running. running along the track, hoping to make it to the next stop before a train came by and flattened me. before a train zoomed by and whisked me off and threw me under the tracks and shredded me.

all of which couldn't have been any worse than if those six huge, blond, white men had whisked me off into an alley (if they thought they should bother, that is) and raped me, for being a woman walking around the old city admiring the architecture, or for being a woman walking home carrying three bags of groceries, or for being a woman walking around the old city HATING THE ARCHITECTURE it wouldn't matter to them.

but the point is (because there always is) the point is that if i had been caught in the cave of the subway i would have been able to stay alive, unshredded, by squeezing against one of those cutouts they have along the wall. there is one of those little spaces every so often just big enough for a person, that looks so much like the cutout space along a church wall, where st. anthony fits in, or the virgin—

the point is (there must always be a point) that if i had been trapped in the cave of the subway, i would have been able to survive. the point is that even in an unlikely place for a human being, such as the cave of the subway, men have made little st. anthony spaces for people to step into just in case they happen to be running along while there might be a train coming, threatening to shred them—

the remaining point being (you see, a point did remain) that as i was walking along the incredible streets of the old city, without three grocery bags, without wearing alluring clothes, and without the thought of a man in my whole body, six of them leaped out behind me and quickened their step, started to talk about their pricks, started to laugh, walked around to look at me— i scowled— they didn't like that— i was admiring the architecture— so they let me alone for a block or two because i scowled and their pricks probably shriveled, the poor sensitive, easily shreddable things, and i walked towards a more populated area, but before i could reach it, they were behind me again, figuring that they didn't care whether or not i liked the architecture, or that i scowled, or that i wore unappealing (to pricks, that is) brown pants— they managed to get themselves adjusted to their roles, into their tracks, into their trainlike personalities, and they followed me down the street, around me and behind me, at top speeds, where no one had provided little st. anthony spaces for a person in peril to flatten her body against while the train passed!!

it was my fault.

what right did i have to walk around admiring anything,
without a gun to protect me? without sharp claws and fangs to
shred their dicks off? without fire in my breath to singe their very
souls as they approached me?

i tried to imagine the danger, to weigh rape against death and
my muscles ached. to weigh rape against murder and my vagina
tightened. to weigh rape against death against murder against life
in pain against life in any possible shape against the taste of their
blood in my teeth and my vagina tightened and i sweated and
exuded the most hate i have ever hated and walked resolutely past
the six of them toward the subway station clutching my keys
between my fingers ready to shred skin like i'd been doing it all
my life.

༂ຈ

October 28, 1959

"I've only got a few days before this *hallows eve*. The sign to remind me that it's my turn is that ocher and red sprig of oak that grows before the abandoned barn. It's got to be, because it's the only autumnal color I can see from here.

"If I didn't know it was October in this new town, the barn all covered with ivy, green climbing vines of all kinds, the rain falling and falling, it would all look like summer. Except for the sprig of oak. I'm sure of it. My sisters and I have taken care to hide our ways, and so our language is subtle. Its signs, almost invisible.

"A chill down my back. I've never been the object of presage such as this. I am the one, and I would escape now . . . no. Perhaps I would have escaped this morning, before the rain let up enough to show me how the colors grow from ocher to gold to red, on the leaves of the single oak branch that stands before the green vines.

"Deep within the hills the church bells toll the new time of day, before it has been decreed for time to save an hour of daylight before winter. And, so, the town will live an hour longer tonight. But here, in our house away from the valley, the sound of the bells barely reaches us. We are foreigners among the locals, though our ancestors have inhabited this continent for centuries. The air feels heavy on this grey afternoon, the wind hurries on the darkness, the candles grow brighter beside the window.

"When the clock strikes five an hour early, then, I'll go up into the attic to collect the objects of the spell I'm meant to cast. When I open up the cedar chest of my sister's recollections, and I gather memories in purple petals of dried roses, fading in my hands, little pieces through my fingers, like the promises the young man made to her that crumbled when she touched them with her passion— then, I will feel none of the doubt I feel now, contemplating the prospect of his death beneath my hand.

"It was spring that brought him here, spring that drove him certain to attain my sister's love. She was beautiful at dusk during the summer, when she sat, obediently, yet ignoring our advice. Her cheeks had blushed after our warning: *don't bend your will, retain your heart,* but her lips were determined to receive him.

"The end of the summer made her swelter in her first signs of longing. Her breaths exhaled pain, and she trembled when she sang. Her sweetest voice tasted of honey— golden and heavy was my young sister's desire.

"She slept without dreaming, passing from night to day merely to behold the sight of him again. Her lids lay still on her closed eyes, and we, sisters, watched while the moonlight bathed her.

"It was not in silence that we witnessed the weakening of her spirit. Yet our knowledge was not meant to reach her through words. She had chosen to test her life against the highest of all risks; she gave her heart to another and received emptiness in return.

91

"Now, she must travel alone and in pain, as she regains her strength. To fill up the void he created in her, she must grow complete: all of her must be inhabited by herself alone. She must feel no hope, be bound by no ties, before she can grow free again.

"She has gone, then, from this house on the first of October, and we sisters await the news of her triumph or death to reach us in a year's time. The old songs are clear. We know that a man of this land who has taken the heart of a witch cannot live if she is to survive. There must be no hope to bind her will to his. Only in death shall a such a man release his hold of her love.

"The bells toll faintly, and the clock echoes with its chime. It is time to prepare the thorn that, on all hallows eve, will pierce the hand of the man. He will feel the sting as he dances and courts the maidens in town. I shudder and reel. I curse my own fate. The red sprig of oak points toward my window; it bends in the rain. I must rise then, and prepare to avenge.

"Inside the deep cedar chest, I'll smell the dried roses she kept from his gifts and touch the smooth satins she wore for his smiles, and I'll taste all the tears she swallowed in silence; slowly, I'll brew up the poison. In three days' time, at midnight on *hallows eve*, he will die."

❧

Soy un ser de otro planeta. *I say it because there is no other way to explain it.* Mi madre nos envió como arañitas flotando por las aguas a sus millares de hijas, a salvarse donde pudiesen. *My mother sent us like little spiders floating over the waters, all her thousands of daughters, to save ourselves wherever we could. And we saved ourselves, most of us, while many perished or barely survive from a perilous addiction.* Estar adicta es peligroso para los extraterrestres, para las arañas que tienen que vivir de incognito. *Addictions are dangerous for extraterrestrials, for the spiders who must live incognito.* A veces las arañas quedan adictas al dolor que es como una luz cristalina que les come las entrañas. *Sometimes spiders end up addicted to pain, to sorrow that is like a crystalline light that eats through her life's blood.*

Sin embargo, sí. I am the daughter of a comet from a southern latitude that extends its tail between two oceans and then is lost, disintegrating in a thousand islands glowing in the night. *Soy hija de un cometa en una latitud austral que extiende su cola entre dos océanos y después se pierde, pulverizándose en miles de islitas luminosas que alumbran de noche.* I don't remember my mother because she sealed the heart of each daughter before she sent us out in the world, shipwrecked, but I remember what she transmitted to me

93

telepathically: Go find sprawling cities, a metropolis where each one can pass unnoticed, where one can live crocheting webs, and always, always, we must be near the sea. *A mi madre no la recuerdo. Me selló el corazón, antes de enviarnos por el mundo de náufragas. Que buscáramos ciudades amplias, una metrópolis en donde poder pasar desapercibida, donde poder vivir tejiendo redes, y siempre, siempre, con acceso al mar.*

Rivers flank my existence in this city. I spend my days unaware of their currents, yet my sanity depends on knowing, somewhere in some submerged part of me, that my soul has access to their waters, beyond their urban banks, to the oceans. On full moon nights, I sit alone near the piers, reaching across the waters to commune with my sisters. Each standing on her own pier, shore, or river's edge, we extend outward our spiders' webs until our thoughts meet and our spirits touch once more.

Years ago, when we were fledgling weavers, newly arrived, when our memories had not adjusted to hold all that we needed to know in this new land, there were times when I could not remember all of myself or what my mission was. I heard messages, now and then, from older sister immigrants who tried to leave me clues, gently, to bring me back to the fold. It was a woman selling parsley in Chinatown who slipped some magic herbs into my bag. They did not look like much at first, just some dried leaves I could not identify. And once, it was woman wearing a policeman's uniform who touched my shoulder and looked into my eyes while I waited on the platform, for a train.

Later, I did not see the messengers, only their signs left at my door step, a leaf, a piece of thread from one of their webs, a small stone shaped like a heart. I knew they were calling me, and I learned to listen, especially at night.

Once I recognized myself as a spider all my mother's memories became my own, and my consciousness began to extend beyond the shores of the rivers, beyond the edges of the harbor. In those days I was no longer ashamed of being small and brown, of having arrived from far away and for speaking another tongue. I understood all the words that people spoke to me, and as I learned to weave webs, small ones at first, small ones I could hide under my dress, my power manifested itself in everything I did. There were small bits of power that glowed and followed me when I moved and would sometimes, reveal me to the earthbound. I started leaving my doorway only in the evenings, then, because the glow of my power would be diffused by the lights of the city. My mother, that distant flickering spider lost in a shower of meteorites, knew very well what to do. She hadn't neglected anything when she let us go.

But this existence has not been easy for everyone; in fact, it has been a battle for me to keep my soul. For other sisters, it has meant death.

In time, and perhaps quite significantly when times were hard, when my work was rejected, when the earthbound reacted with envy and secretly coveted the strength that guided me, and I was aimless again, looking for another job, another place to live, that is when I learned to see the others.

They appeared to everyone else like earthbound women, sometimes with children, sometimes alone. I learned to recognize them because of the distance in their eyes, the hunger in their hands. They could not weave. They could not create enough energy to lift themselves above earthly pain and so were bound by it, addicted in its cycle, craving the glow of freedom our extraterrestrial ancestors had known.

As time went by I, too, gave birth to a child. I tried to raise his little soul to the stars, to teach him how to soar with us in the black interstellar night, but it would not be granted to me. My own soul had been captured after all, and I had not enough power to save my son. He would grow up earthbound while I watched him from a distance, always weaving for him a spell of safety that at least he would grow fully even if far away from the love radiating from my spider's heart. When my second child was born, a girl this time, I had nothing more to give, my webs lay dusty, half buried in the earth. She, with the huge eyes of the newborn, watched me weave frantically, attempt flight in the pale glow that emanated from within me, barely able to keep us alive.

When the moon grows full, many creatures change, take on new shapes, and are freed from their former ghost selves. So it was with me and my daughter, and many of the spiders who languished half hidden in penumbra. When the moon is full, night becomes thick, and the light of the stars that brought us here fills us once more, yet there lies the paradox: it is in the darkness that we attain our full power. When I understood this fully, I learned to approach the others who were lost.

At first, they spoke in anguish and confusion, and refused my help in anger. They did not wish to be spiders any more. They denied their birthplace, our mother, our journey to this world. At times, these errant spiders damned their own name and spoiled the course of my webs. I invoked our mother's warnings, pleaded with them to return, to no avail. In the still night, the ripple of water hitting the pier, I would suddenly come back to earthly consciousness, having lost the connection to the webs.

On nights like these, I wandered by the black water of the river, gathering strength from the deep velvet of the sky, and willed myself to call a meeting of the sisters who live in cities near to each other. As the day descended, I covered my face and my arms, hurrying home to sleep, avoiding well-traveled streets and the peering looks of the earthbound.

In the days that followed, my webs were growing tangled. I slept by day and worked by night, suffering sharp pains in my abdomen, in my head, in my fingertips. Memories of my childhood in my distant home flooded my waking hours, my dreams.

I suspect that each of us, in our own way, wants to abandon the sisterhood of the web. We have all but stopped speaking the language of our mother, and more and more, we have adopted the ways of the earthbound. Anger swells within me, impotence. I can't live alone without the web. When I try to hold fast and blame the disintegration of our souls on the vices of the earthbound, they call me crazy, old-fashioned, willful, and unwilling to forgive. As night falls again, I light my candles and ignore their voices in my head.

Before the next moon, I prepare to walk the piers at night, to call the older spiders to come to me and aid me in this quest. But one day, before I begin, a young woman I barely remember comes to my home and surprises me out of my reveries. She walks in, her long brown legs enveloped in colorful pants, so tall and bronzed that it seems she has lived in the sun forever. She wears gold blouses and scarves, and her hair is braided under a webcrown of red velvet. She looks strange to me and I look strange to her, wearing my traditional black, my hair long and woven. "Sister!" she calls to me, as though imagining that I am asleep, not acknowledging my spider's somnolent stance. "What are these!", she shouts and picks up my webs with her hands, only to drop them and run to the windows to throw them open, as if the air was not enough for her. She has shattered my peace.

My sister's love is receding, a shallow tide going further from my arms. I can't hold her, and yet her attention to my life is suffocating. She wakes me when I sleep, insists that I eat the food she cooks for me, and keeps me from weaving while she tells me her long stories. I can't follow them. There is something she wants me to know, but I can't hear it. My sister, for I have come to believe she really is my sister, confuses me, she scares me, and she shocks me by denying what I know to be true. "Look," she says pointing to some strange portraits she has in a book. "There are only the two of us. There are no webs, and there are no moonlit piers. Wake up!" She wants to take me into the sunlight, not acknowledging that sun would mean death for an old spider like me.

When the moon is full again, I know my sister loves me still, though I have been crying after a very long time, and unable to weave. She has said very cruel things to me. I have told her that my son will be at the pier. "No," she said. "Your son is gone; he is a man now, in another place, far away from here. Don't grieve for him." "And, my daughter—" I try to tell her. "No," she says. "Your daughter is dead. Let her go."

At night, she has consented to come to the pier. A ritual, she calls it, but I am certain that once she feels the voices of all the daughters of the comet radiating through the web, she will remember. She hasn't stopped talking today, and I think I understand. She loves the earthbound women as she would a spouse. She wants to be united with one of them, but she promises not to leave the sisterhood. She even attempted to weave with me at dawn, to prepare for tonight's communication. "I understand," she has told me. She, too, was looking for a home for her soul.

But now that we are here by the water, she seems nervous. She looks around. Is she afraid of earthbound people finding us here? I assure her this will not happen. It is safe here by the river, but her eyes dart back and forth along the water's edge. Her web, I don't know where she has hidden it, but I am certain once the moon rises she will produce it and extend it over the water. Behind me, the lights of the city seem brighter. I reach for my sister's hand to prepare ourselves and I sense her fear. I will try to find her web, I think, and I ask her to begin spitting, to let her weaving become automatic and rhythmic, the way I learned when I was young. "No," she says. "I don't know what you mean." And she pulls away while the clouds clear away and reveal the moon, full and bright at its zenith.

I bring my webs forward, bend to stretch them wide across the water. I spit and salivate luxuriously to show her the way, but she retreats. I can feel the call of the others, already. I want her to hear, to feel with me, but she doesn't respond. She looks frightened, angry, and as I weave toward her again, I see the other woman, an earthbound female extending her own arms to envelop me. "Stop!" I scream at her. "Leave me and my sister alone!" But there is no time. The tide has risen. The moon is full and powerful, calling me, calling us, and I must return to the webs. I pull and throw, push out the call and receive the words, in my bones, in my veins, but I forget what they say. I hear the boats on the river, the cars on the highway, and many voices behind me, but not across the water. I know what has happened. The earthbound woman has taken my sister away, and she has severed the connection. A man has joined them. He and the woman wear odd uniforms. I see them, now, standing together, pulling my webs away as though they were garbage, throwing them in my grocery cart, and leading me away from the water. "No," I tell them. I try to sound mysterious and knowledgeable. I try to frighten them, but the woman is strong. She lifts me up and puts me in her car. "It will be alright," she says to me. I don't know why, but I believe her. I'm tired and perhaps it's time to put the webs away for the winter. "Yes, " I say, "it will be alright," but I can't keep my eyes open anymore. I let myself be led away, asleep, because I don't want to hear anymore, and yet I ache. I throb. My head, my abdomen, my fingertips . . ., and my younger sister is crying.

&

This is the story of Jacinta, the witch who knew my great grandmother Chillpila, and who communed with ghosts in her old ship, a creaky schooner anchored in a rugged cove of the southern Chilean archipelago below the island of Chiloé. Perhaps this is also the story of the great Indian witch Chillpila who was known for changing shapes, and for grounding in dry land the ship of the Spaniard Moraleda, when he attempted to match his powers with hers in 1787. She was the ancestor for whom my great grandmother was named.

Nobody really knows how witchcraft came to the region, but it is well documented that there is a school of witchcraft in Chiloé, and a male witch who is the king of Quicaví, or the kingdom of Santiago. It is also well known, if never mentioned, that the men fear the memory of Chillpila, and jealously guard the secret of their arts in the cave of Quicaví.

Jacinta met my great grandmother in 1939, when she was only 25, and Chillpila was at least 90. Even though Jacinta had lived all her life in the islands, she knew very little about the witches, something not at all unusual for the majority of people in this region. Jacinta was an orphan from the island of Quinchao, who had never married and had no children. She was a weaver who traveled from island to island with her portable loom, settling down for a few weeks in a woman's home when she was hired to weave blankets for the winter. In the summer, she tanned animal hides and sold them off the piers to the crew of the many cargo ships, often little better than sea pirates, passing through the archipelago.

But I won't tell you about the routine of Jacinta's life, rather the event that changed it, one cloudless day in November, when she was sequestered aboard a smugglers' schooner, and attacked by godless, treacherous bandits, whom she fought bravely for her life. It was there that she met the ghost. Unable to shake it away, she sailed the old ship to the port of Quicaví at dawn and wandered the streets dressed in the pirates' clothes, until some old women found her and directed her to the hut of the witch Chillpila, my great grandmother.

Doña Chillpila did look like the frail old woman everyone expected her to be, gray and stooped with corrugated features that never smiled, but her eyes were shiny black and she moved swiftly without anybody's help. She dragged the spooked Jacinta into the hut, sat her down on a sheepskin rug, and gave her a steaming gourd of strong mate made with goatsmilk and loaded with brown sugar.

Some people said that Doña Chillpila moved so fast because she was so good at turning herself into an owl; that she was three hundred years old, and was hardly human anymore. To Jacinta she did seem like an owl, sitting very still in front of her, puffing from time to time on her red clay pipe.

"The ghost has come for you," pronounced Doña Chillpila before Jacinta could utter a word. "She was thrown from the

102

lighthouse last night at the same time the smugglers took you away in their ship. This ghost was a witch who wants to claim your body."

"How do you know about the ship, how do you know?" kept asking Jacinta who was terrified, but Chillpila only pointed behind her to the pale yellow cloud that formed around Jacinta's dark, bedraggled form. The fire sputtered under the iron kettle, the witch Chillpila pulled on her pipe.

"Look," said the witch. "Listen, the ghost speaks."

A sound like rain or like embers hissing began to fill the room. Closing her eyes, lowering her thin brown face until her chin rested on the brass buttons of her black coat, Jacinta listened.

The pain was white, white like a burst of light that overcame me and then it passed. I don't know who threw me into the sea, against the rocks. I only know they weren't women's hands. My head was shattered, my body plunging in the furious tide, in the coldest bluegreen water I had ever seen, or that I'd ever felt, drowning me before the shreds of my cranium and my dark chestnut braids floated up among the algae and the air bubbles next to my face.

The gulls dove to the rocks to pick at the debris, while I rose up from the sea. I spirit, I soul, unraveling from sea tendrils, air bubbles, I floated easily among the waves and was lost at dawn with the sharp cries of the gulls.

I saw a golden thread among the waves that carried me towards the ship, groaning with the weight of old wood, moth-eaten mast and sails. Rising inside the ship, I saw your face, bruised and pale with terror, grasping a dagger in your hand, the body of a man at your feet, mujer pirata, and my presence reflected in your black eyes.

The shimmering fog that was the ghost quivered once and was gone. In the witch's house, the day was full, and the sunshine streamed across the dusty floor, the rug where Jacinta and the witch sat, and the white goat sleeping by the cold chimney. The witch woke from her trance and prepared to light her pipe,

103

holding it greedily with her gnarled hands, sucking the red clay tip while her eyes closed again and rested from the effort.

Jacinta looked at her black coat and leather leggings as though for the first time, shaking her head, looking again towards the spot where the image of the ghost had just faded.

"When I recovered from the beating and the ache in my bones, I took these clothes from the first pirate I killed," she told Chillpila. The old woman nodded; the young woman stood on shaking legs and agve vent to her anger.

"He was the one who raped me, cut my hair with a knife, and left me naked to die. With his knife in my hand, I went to find the other three who had left the scumbreath in charge of me. I fought them hand-to-hand with a strength I had never felt before. They jumped overboard, and I left them to find their own way to shore; then I threw the body of my tormentor to the fishes."

Dona Chillpila reached for the young woman's hand, and admonished her, accompanied by nods and quick pulls of tobacco from her pipe.

"You have spilled blood, m'hija. "Now, the judges must put you to death. But if you escape death, the ghost will take you. You must become a more powerful witch. I can help you."

"But I don't want to be a witch!" Jacinta looked at Doña Chillpila with sad eyes, her short hair crowning her young face, pleading for help.

"You can take the soul of an animal, or of one of the dead pirates-- pero bruja eres, hija mía."

Pacing the dusty floor, Jacinta grew more accustomed to the thick leather boots and the freedom of men's pants. She thought that some day she may smoke a clay pipe like the witch's pipe.

Finally, she asked: "How can I take the soul of one of those . . . pirates? All I want is to forget all this."

Doña Chillpila nodded and finally smiled, nodded and smiled, knowing at once what Jacinta was thinking. "You have killed many a goat and tanned its hide for your survival. Your struggle on that ship was also for your survival. It won't be hard for you to find a mountain lion on the island of Chaulinec; go there with the ship. Take your knife, and follow my voice."

There was no rest for Jacinta once she returned to the ship after stalking the mountain lion all night. Even in the coves the waters of the Pacific are restless. The tide lashed at the rocks and folded in upon itself, rocking the ship like a walnut. Dumping the yellow hide of the animal in a heap, Jacinta hoisted the anchor overboard, and secured the sails the best way she could. Exhausted, she climbed into the rank blankets of the captain's bunk, the cleanest place in the whole schooner, and tried to sleep. No sooner did she close her eyes that she was plunged into heavy sleep, while a yellow luminescence enveloped her. In a few minutes, the ghost of the murdered witch sat heavily upon Jacinta's chest, waking her, though no longer frightening her.

"Let me sleep, cruel ghost," Jacinta begged.

"Your body belongs to me, mujer pirata," whistled the ghost, a pale Indian face with sad features, long braids draping over a blood-streaked gown.

Jacinta did not resist. Who was she to argue with a ghost? Doña Chillpila had warned her not to commune with the ghost after midnight, but she had no knowledge of these arts. The ghost was there, on top of her, demanding the use of her body. She was a fugitive herself and a thief, though she felt no guilt over her actions. Being a witch might be easier this way after chasing a mountain lion with a knife.

105

Unsure whether she dreamed or not, Jacinta opened the black coat, unlaced her woolen shirt, and bared her breasts to the ghost.

"Ahhhhh . . ." the ghost seemed to exhale with satisfaction, and Jacinta slid the leggings off her body until she lay naked under the luminous apparition.

Fifty three years have passed. The name of Jacinta has grown into a legend as haunting as that of Chillpila. In the archipelago fog rises like steam above islands or beans in a churning, primordial soup. When the fog clears, the blue Pacific bathes the coasts of each island, a green jewel reborn in the sunlight.

Among the people, interest in witchcraft peaks and wanes; researchers come from the universities, publish their theses, and leave again. The dangerous turf wars among witches, like the one that caused the death of the witch in the lighthouse, are a thing of the past. Times are hard, and these days witches merely fly at night or change shapes when they need to travel from island to island.

But Jacinta was one witch with a social conscience as well as a sense of humor. In the 50s and 60s she was involved in the Indigenous uprisings of the southern regions. Wearing her usual black leather men's clothes and puffing on a red clay pipe, she was often seen at night near the bars where smugglers, sailors, and government informers drank. A thick fog followed the informers who would be found in a ditch covered by leeches. Nothing rankled the male witches more, though, than knowing that Jacinta was a favorite with the women. It seems she had a special enchantment to arouse women as they sang in church or as they went about their household chores, sometimes to the point of a most unholy ecstasy.

She was persecuted for years by the authorities during the dictatorship, but it was very simple for Jacinta to blend in as an old woman and make people believe she had died. It was in this guise that I finally saw her, on the coast of Chaulinec, almost five years ago to the day.

I am Chillpila's descendant, it's true, but my mother and grandmother had never told me anything about her, hoping to break the cycle of witchcraft in our line. Still, it was no surprise when I stood gazing into the horizon that day, hypnotized by the roaring surf of the Pacific, until I saw Jacinta's old schooner rounding the cove, sails billowing and snapping. The sea lions barked and dove off the rocks to meet the ship, and I followed them into the cold water because I knew that after all these years, that old pirate witch Jacinta had come for me.

❧

107

When I managed to slide closed the plexigate, I was gasping for breath. For the moment, I wanted to keep out the bloated, ulcerous limbs of the *touched ones*. I was depleted and shocked. Back in Venezuela City, none of us ever guessed it would be so sad here. Naturally, my people and I are not naive enough to think of the northern continent as that glowing, polished "land of opportunity," as it was known in the 20th century. Still, we somehow imagined their Elder government would have dealt more sensibly with the Disease.

Below the cell I occupy, the touched ones still crawl around in the semi-darkness, trying to climb up the side of the cellblocks and gain access to open cellgates which might provide a safe place for sleep. When I arrived today, the cellblock keeper warned me not to open the plexigate unless I wanted to step out onto the walkway, but I disregarded the warning. I wanted to breathe some air, even though the air in the whole city feels used up, tired. Instead, I was surrounded by three touched ones wrapped in rags, horribly deformed and malodorous. I tried my chants and reached for their auras, but these humans barely had a thin layer of grayish light around their physical bodies. There was hardly any psychic energy for me to contact, and their brains were completely atrophied by malnutrition and the ravages of the Disease. We could not communicate.

When I failed to help them, they retreated onto the electronic walkway which connects my cell to the others, perhaps physically exhausted and shocked by my vital energy. I shut the plexigate and leaned against it, feeling suddenly as exhausted as they, whispering some Blessingway mantras to myself. The depleted auras of those touched ones saddens me.

It's very windy out there, and there is a red glow in the sky. At first, I thought this was the urban village called Chicago in the 1990s, but it isn't. It's one that was thought to be uninhabited by mid-21st century; this is old New York town.

Though I was never very interested in ancient world history, I needed to learn quickly about this continent which looms almost forbidden in the dark North sea. I am a curandesa in my native land, a profession that evolved rapidly since the first decades of the Disease, particularly in what used to be called Third World zones. Curandesas are a combination of old world doctors, healers, counselors, acupuncturists, and medicine women, though there are some men curandesas. We practice hypnosis through rituals we learned from the western Indians who fled the northern continent in 2005. It is the only way we can control the deadliest side-effect of the Disease: Fear. Yet, living in our sheltered healing community, I had no conception of the ravaged condition of human beings in this place, ever since the northern continent cut itself off from the rest of the globe.

It was surprising, then, when we heard talk of a vaccine cure being developed in the northern continent. I was sent from Venezuela City to investigate.

109

Many times before, members of the Global Association of Curandesas sent emissaries to different parts of the globe after rumors sprang up of a new cure being developed. The rumors spread just after a new strain of the virus had decimated another community. Some of us suspected unethical experimentation and were opposed to sending emissaries. Because emissaries were unfamiliar with local history, they were manipulated by political factions and rarely learned anything of value. In 2273 it was rumored that two Palestinian emissaries were diverted to the northern continent and never returned to their zone.

I was advised to learn as much as I could first, about the area of the northern continent I would be visiting. I started by researching the bibliofiles, but ended up having to pay memorizers to talk to me, or just borrowing memory chips from our association contacts. Since the Computer Down-age of the 2240s, not only did all space travel cease forever, but the global system of information and communication also broke down. Apparently, it was done intentionally through the introduction of a virus which, ironically, duplicated in computers the effect of the Disease in human beings. From that time on, bibliofiles contain everything ever written, but unclassified.

There is no way of knowing what is fact, fiction, film reviews, plays, re-enactments, documentary broadcasts, hologram transmissions, simulated news events— human history is complete chaos.

In the past forty years, while technicians all over the globe have strived to reorganize information systems, it has become apparent that human populations have very short memories. Some educationists attribute this to our shorter life spans since the Disease, our greater degree of specialization in tasks, our lowered resistance to stress. Whatever the reason, the fact is that

110

we have forgotten. My generation knows nothing that is not transmitted through our specific tasks; our view of human history is not linked, and neither is our global data banks.

The red glow in the sky seems to be dimmer. I hear it is never really dark in this village, that the mercury illuminators glow perpetually because it is never really light. Through the plexigate, I can still distinguish vague the shapes, the eroded architecture of the 20th century. I have no access to any history before that. There is a great iron structure that extends across a foul gorge they call the East River. It carries no current, but it isn't exactly empty. It seems to be a repository for centuries of refuse. The enormous crane dangles an iron cage from what used to be a track, perhaps. It carried people from one side to the other of this fetid river.

On the other side, I see the only remaining building to tower above the myriad concrete cellblocks with plexigates and narrow access to the electronic walkways that connect the maze of rounded structures. That building is rectangular. The top of it seems to have been sliced off at a 45 degree angle. It is now covered by pleximirror, and a greenish light emanates from it into the humid twilight. Some historical accounts indicate that this building was originally the Bank of the City, and that it was built to look like a big box with the top chopped off. But most historians think this is popular lore making a legend out of some disaster, possibly the earthquakes of the 2010s.

Of course, if we really look at ourselves, we are all *touched ones*, since every human being on the globe has carried the antibody for the Disease since the year 2015. In fact, I have learned from my recent historical research that the Great Infection of those early times began in the northern continent. It was the first time in recorded history that an Elder government, originally benevolent popular councils, actually turned against its own people. More radical voices have claimed that it wasn't the first time it was done, merely the first time recorded.

It was a strange period of sleep that lasted about six hours. These cells, I realized, are not really made of cement, but rather, a mixture of granite, molten metal, cement, organic material, wood, and thousands of other particles processed and reshaped after several nuclear meltdowns, earthquakes, laser blastings, and many other urban catastrophes. In my sleep I absorbed much information from these rounded walls and the faint energy left behind by sickly humans who have preceded me.

As I descended to the lower level to find the main electronic walkway, the cellkeeper seemed surprised to see me about at that hour. She offered me some breakfast ration that was included in the price of the cell, but the food she held toward me in a gray plastic tray, was dead. Certainly, the ration had caloric value, but nothing emanated from it. It might as well have been the same gross putty used to build the cellblocks. The stranger thing, though, was that she refused my offer of live food. The seeds and fruit I held in my hands glowed with energy. I looked at the woman's frail form, her barely yellow aura, and wondered how she managed to move as quickly as she did when she seemed so taxed.

Skating off on the walkway, I resolved to offer the cellblock keeper my services for a healing. I had been warned not to reveal my craft during my travels, but it seemed ugly not to share what I could.

In order to find the cure, or at least, to obtain information about the latest developments, I needed to make contact with the northern continent physicians. Upon my arrival, I had been told they would be meeting today in a medical college. As I neared the large complex of rounded cellblocks, the electronic emissions forming the walkway suddenly weakened and broke off, and several dazed people plummeted to their deaths. I had just then come hovering over a window ledge and I grabbed onto it while the rays of the walkway dissipated into the constant rain.

Frozen to the side of the building, I waited to feel the spirits rising from the bodies below. Slowly, a gray veil of delicate shadow floated by me. Most human beings in this village seem on the verge of death. There isn't much energy even left to die. I slid down to the street level and talked with survivors and touched ones who stood about. It was common, they said. At that hour of the morning, the power often gave way, when only transients, touched ones, and thieves would be traveling anyway. I looked at the reddish sky through the misty rain, and sensed the brightening of the sky by degrees. Perhaps this was daylight. I got my bearings and headed to the entrance of the college. Behind me, the bodies of the dead remained untouched.

§

The Chief Physician at the Medical College appeared to me like no curandesa I had ever seen. As I approached the large domed structure, her large face loomed suddenly above me. Her bulging eyes scrutinized me, and I sensed her identity and questions before she spoke. I jumped with surprise before I realized that it was her image projected into a hologram that I had seen, several times her size, hovering over the entrance and peering into everybody's face as they arrived. We stood transfixed, newspeople, researchers and physicians from other zones, in a semi-circle until the real Chief Physician walked in through a round door to our right.

113

She was a very lightskinned, stocky human, quite short in stature, wearing a grey suit with the letters "CP" on her lapel. Her aura was the yellowish gray I had become accustomed to seeing, but she glowed with a thin blue luminescence all around. Attended by solemn-faced male humans dressed in blue uniforms, the CP directed us through the laboratories. The attendants glowed with the same two-toned aura. She spoke in a nasal, metallic voice, and displayed for us the experiments and their results. The attendants, who appeared to be both researchers and guards, insisted that we look at the slides under powerful electron microscopes and compare previously diseased tissue with completely healthy samples. Documentation for the data was presented in hologram displays of stunning quality, with images so sharp they appeared practically solid. Suddenly, I detected a rise in my temperature, and a tingling sensation in my spine. I attempted to leave the main area where the holograms were projected, but I was prevented by the CP herself.

"You can only get the full effect by standing here, Curandesa." Her thin hands kept me from moving, her arms extended, as though she did not wish to get too close to me.

I studied the faces of the other guests. They seemed intent on the explanations, the newspeople with their headsets busily recording into holocorders, the researchers and physicians whispering comments into their memory chips. I found the experiments inconclusive, merely replicating old methods of isolating viral strains. I began to suspect a ruse, another reason for wanting this specific group of humans in this location.

As soon as I felt everyone's attention to be concentrated on the next set of holograms, I retreated through the corridors until I came to the main plexigate. Feeling overheated still, I headed towards a public liquid dispenser and reached for a bottle of water. Then, thinking of the proximity of this dispenser to the college, I reached instead into my satchel and popped a few water capsules in my mouth. I was beginning to feel intensely distrustful of all services for humans in this continent. With these doubts and some nebulous theories going around in my head, I wanted to search for answers rather than this elusive cure.

Traveling swiftly again on the walkways, I learned to discern the possible breaks in current that had caused the fatal accident earlier that day. Near the "edges" of the sheet of electronic emissions which formed the walkways, there were almost imperceptible blue sparks. If one sensed these short circuits, or saw them, the way I could, one could stop in plenty of time or take an alternate route. No longer in danger of falling, I went to the central bibliofiles where medical data banks could be found.

A domed structure received me, and I quickly found the sonic lift that would take me to the appropriate data banks. I adjusted my memory chip to receive even my most subtle telepathic messages. In this manner, I could think and research at the same time. My notes would be edited later, when I returned home.

The CP continued to intrigue me and make me extremely uneasy. As I searched through the disks, my temperature continued to rise. None of the representatives I had seen was a curandesa. This fact in itself was not surprising. Many researchers from europa, and certainly from this continent, were devoted solely to cures by chemical means, and had not yet learned to heal themselves by other disciplines, such as ours. What was unusual was the complete absence of healers of any type in the files I was reviewing, and yet I had not sensed the progress of the disease in the CP or her attendant researchers. In fact, I had sensed nothing familiar, just that thin blue luminescence.

The news files had no data on northern continent medical cures or advances for years. I sifted through commercial news. Nothing. I switched to historical files, and tried to avoid the novelizations. This zone had copious records of that type, and I synthesized the basic facts into my chip.

"At the beginning of the 21st century it was difficult to know which was the greater threat to humankind— poverty, hunger, war, or the Disease. Third world zones were denied access to clean blood and immunization. This was long before humans could mutate to adapt to certain aspects of the Disease, and having the virus meant almost certain death. A peculiar migration had begun at the end of the 20th century. Humans from Latin America, Africa, and certain parts of Asia strove in great numbers to reach the northern continent and europa. Editorialized versions maintain that this was due to the systematic plunder of the Third world by the First, and people simply went to reclaim the resources they had lost. In europa, the middle east, and the soviet zones, a wave of unprecedented political freedom gave birth to the first Elder governments, a council of benevolent humans who answered only to their own people . . .".

Files on the great infection were seriously jumbled. I did find valuable records which confirmed the annihilation of all neighboring zones by the northern continent. The files traced the Indian migration of 2005 to that time, when all the northern Indian nations migrated to the zone then known as Macchu Picchu and its surroundings. "The first known cures for the Disease were created in these new villages. There were Asian herbs, laser technology, Navajo hypnosis, Mapuche chants, hatha yoga, and zen cleansings of all negative energy. Telepathy and biofeedback made giant leaps forward. Meanwhile, the northern continent medical establishment swarmed the southern zone trying to lay claim to knowledge that was given freely to everyone who needed it.

"In 2010, many earthquakes decimated areas of the globe. Parts of the northern continent were washed to sea, and the crisis again brought repression and hoarding of resources. Brownskinned human beings were persecuted; many were exiled, and a reverse migration took place: to India, to Nigeria, Venezuela, Brazil, Central China. Earthquakes continued to plunge islands and parts of continents into the ocean until 2015, when there was finally calm, but it was also discovered that reactionary factions all over the globe had begun the great infectation in an effort to control the remaining resources. The new regime of the northern continent preached abstention from sexual contact, pointing to the great numbers of brownskinned human beings as evidence that the globe's resources were unfairly taxed by those who bred too quickly and too plentifully. Brownskinned women were believed to be parthenogenic. Autosexual practice was the only kind of activity legally permitted. The Brownskinned were blamed for the transmission of the Disease and the now clearly despotic regime sought to control its spread by testing every human being with brown skin for the antibody. The cruelly ironic result was that, as the Disease and famine spread through the globe, no human being ever willingly desired to have sex any longer. Experiments were conducted on human beings who were used to incubate serum after serum, while the great progress healers were making in other parts of the globe was ignored.

"As the decades passed, there seemed to be no way to stem the disasters, but eventually the population reached a stabilization point in 2210. Small mutations started to appear. Mutated human beings have few teeth as adults, little hair, four digits on our feet, and those females who are fertile have multiple births. We are not subject to many infections, but we can smell only strong odors, and we are very near sighted. We don't need as much food, but then we can only taste 10% of what we consume, and finally, our life span is only 50.3 years."

History. This collection of pathetic facts makes up our current reality. I am glad I am not a historian, or even a teacher. Healing is good work, effective, and it keeps one very busy. My lower back was aching terribly, so I loaded the last disk into my chips and closed down the main computer.

§

It was night again. The sky glowed a dark red and the mist became more dense. Exiting the domed archives, I traveled south to my cell. Avoiding several power breaks, I noticed other people sensed them as well. I sped along on narrower walkways on the west side of the village. Approaching a large open plaza, I joined some younger humans who carried ancient instruments for musical entertainment. Electronic saxophones and keyboards bounced with clearly detectible energy. While the musicians played, I touched their auras from a safe distance and taught them telepathically to reconstruct their body cells. They would be almost healed by morning and would surely live a long time. Two women danced, embracing each other tenderly. On the ground, attracted by the intense energy, touched ones who were beyond any healing crawled. Those who could still walk kicked the others along the ground, forcing them away from the circle of light and music that had been created. I felt more tired and consumed by worry, still I perceived the glowing of blue, purple, and green auras. There was red iridescence and orange bursts of human sensuality.

Immersed in the music, I gazed for a time at the faintly discernible full moon until, feeling unbearably feverish, I dumped my small satchel on the ground and distributed the dried fruit and seeds I carried, but I ate little, delighting instead in the appetite of these northern humans. I passed around the small flask of ginseng liqueur and watched their faces glow. Outside the circle, other touched ones moaned hopelessly.

The music continued, and I remained on the ground, tired, but able now to review the last of the information. Some children attempted to rob me, but finding nothing of worth in my pockets, they sat quietly, holding my arms, my legs, my feet.

Though I read quickly through the information on the miniature screen of my memorychip, I felt, with a tightening of my stomach, that I already knew what I would learn: Murder as *population control*. Wholesale genocide accomplished through simple means. Through fingerprint verifiers. Inoculations. Mass blood testing. Poisoned water. Nerve gas at demonstrations, outdoor concerts, hologram transmissions. The cruelty was staggering. Now I knew what attacked the blood in my veins at that very moment. My bone marrow duplicated mutant cells and shot my body with pain. This was no longer the Disease alone, but massive immunodeficiency from many viral combinations.

Realizing I had already discharged much of my energy, I knew I had little time to concentrate on saving myself. Moving slowly and carefully, I left the park and tried to find the walkway that would lead me back to my cellblock. I had been irradiated through the holograms at the medical college. The macabre procedure was undetectable and was probably an effective way to kill within days. At least, I knew ways to retard the process.

119

Slowly, I drew in my breath and directed it outward, rhythmically as I skated. My strong body might survive this onslaught, but not so the others who had undoubtedly been irradiated. Why? To neutralize any efforts to spread the information on the cure research? No. There was no research on the cure, only experimentation on new methods of death. The college was the link to the Elder government and its complicated network of population control. Information on ongoing research was released periodically to obscure the systematic destruction of unwanted humans, and when curious researchers arrived from other zones, they had to be killed.

Arriving at the cellblock, I quickly loaded all my data into the laptop connector I had brought, a sort of "hard" disk which could store 500 gigabytes of information. A cold sensation settled into my chest, and I hoped I had not contracted pneumonia, which would certainly slow my recovery. But the coldness was different. Closing my eyes, I located the source. In the cell below, the cellkeeper lay dead. I boarded the sonic lift with caution, but it was no longer necessary. When I entered her cell, she was alone, although someone had obviously been there before and shot her in the chest with a laser. Placing her arms over her chest, closing her lids, I tried to understand the cause of her death, angrily realizing it was my own presence. The college or the elders, perhaps the CP herself, must have sent someone in looking for me. This woman died in my place. With my eyes closed again, I could summon vague images of her attacker, which revealed it had been a man in a blue suit, unmistakably one of the CP's attendants. Opening my eyes, I whispered my apology to her spirit for causing her death and swore to avenge her. Knowing these were strange emotions for a healer, I fought to will the destruction of the disease within me through my own powers. At the same time, I nurtured an extreme hatred for the CP, her minions, and all of the governing body which ruled this sad land. I probably did not have much time left because they must have known I would not stop until I answered my own questions. Sobering myself, I could not control my emotions in the midst of increasing fever. I also knew I could not leave until I destroyed the CP and her death machine.

Before setting off again on the now deserted walkways, I ingested all my supply of herbal immune-balancer and felt an immediate boost of energy. As I skated back towards the college, I gazed at the blue sparks as I avoided them, and was suddenly seized with an idea more chilling than anything I had encountered: The blue of the sparks, the thin blue luminescence around the aura of the CP and the guards. No other humans glowed with such a strange aura. It could only be artificially created by constant electronic re-charging. If they had managed to bombard their own systems with radiation to kill all traces of the disease, they must have weakened themselves to the verge of death. But with a network of electrodes attached to their suits and sending electronic impulses coursing through their bodies, it is possible they could maintain themselves indefinitely. There had to be a remote source of energy somewhere within the complex.

I entered the college through a plexigate intended for the discharge of refuse. Closing my eyes, I guided myself to the sublevels of the complex until I found a labyrinth of corridors leading to an obvious end. Finding the ports which connected my rudimentary hardware with the laboratories within the complex was amazingly simple. The hologram transmitters, the microscopes, the hydrocarbon freezers engaged with my string command to disengage one by one. Attempting to concentrate and avoid errors, I thought lightly about my future actions. It

121

would be easy to commandeer a sky car in the city at this nour. In fact, I could probably find one from the medical college fleet right outside the north wall. Engaging the automatic pilot due south would have me home shortly after dawn, even unconscious.

Finally, with a deep, resonant hum, only the set of electronic generators vibrated in unison. Attaching a connector from my memory chip to the final port, I programmed a shutdown series. As my fever began to recede, my carefully guarded hatred of the CP, the guards, and the elders began to dissipate. In some part of my psyche, I could feel them approaching. Alerted by the sudden drop in power, they advanced like glowing ghosts through the darkened corridors. They all seemed inconsequential then, so unreal and feeble, because at the end of the sequence on my screen their power source would shut off without a sound, and they would all be most certainly dead.

❧

Wanted: The words of a lesbian of color. One of each color. Snap. No experience required but must be proficient at expressing the deep pain of her existence. Snap. Must exemplify the core of her being in poetic English, using syntax we can all understand. Snap. Must be able to make us all feel the weight of the oppression of her people as it relates to her particular culture. Snap.

Note: She must be a lesbian. Snap. She must identify openly as a lesbian. Snap. She should speak about the triple oppression of being queer, snap— colored, snap— and female, snap— but never vary from her lesbian-identified perspective. Snap. Commitment to multiculturalism preferable; snap— grassroots organizing experience a must.

On Broadway, the mid-day traffic was pouring down like an ocean, a fleet of yellow cabs in wavy brush strokes from the heat and the tears behind the woman's glasses. This woman hailed one of the yellow boat-like shapes and got inside. The voice of a young male doctor with rosy, healthy cheeks had just informed her that her mother was in a hospital uptown. Stable, the doctor had said, but badly shaken from the insulin reaction she had suffered on the street. The woman was all the way downtown, making posters and leaflets for another protest march for civil rights, and there was only one way to get uptown. The trick would be in finding it. The cab navigated up Sixth Avenue and then Eighth, dodging and honking its way, getting stuck at 42nd Street with a few hundred other vehicles swimming around the Port Authority Terminal.

There was nothing she could do. It was summer. It was New York.

The woman sat in the cab trying to calm herself. The doctor said her mother had an insulin reaction and couldn't find help soon enough. Her stomach heaved with anger and impotent nausea. Holding her head, she tried not to think about it, and concentrated instead on the fact that somehow her mother got on an ambulance and got herself to the hospital. The traffic cleared, and the cab moved unimpeded for an entire city block. Her mother was safe. She just had to get there and be perfectly calm, competent, able to speak unaccented English because that always gets the best treatment and the most attention from doctors and nurses who have no time to listen to long stories with too many variables.

Unfortunately, the history of her family had always had too many variables. Immigrant stories always do. Immigrants coming through New York before settling down for years in the suburbs of Anytown, U.S.A. For her family, it was the mid-sixties. She and a little sister and brother, following their parents and all their suitcases all the way from their unspecified country, first through Miami International Airport, then through Kennedy Airport, looked obviously like so many FOB's. These days, she cringes to think how they got through those tortuous lines at U.S. Customs, the questions, the checking and double-checking, the waiting, the disdain from the functionaries, the humiliation, the language barrier. Then, there were the gray-green walls of the interrogation cubicle where the parents were questioned, made to wait, questioned again by men in suits with John Wayne eyes who appeared so friendly. She leaned gingerly against the walls, tried to calm the kids who wanted to go to the bathroom in the middle of it all. There was something dangerous in those smiles. Would they be allowed to stay? They only had suitcases now, with books, three records of folk music, a change of clothes for each of them.

The kids were hopping on one foot. She composed sentences out of movie English to ask directions to the bathrooms. Navigating the wide hallways of the airport, she and the kids skated over the polished floors. Being a kid herself, she had forgotten the John-Waynes, and they were off to the next adventure. Were ordinary people friendlier in the sixties? How did they find the bathrooms in the end? Hours later it seemed, standing all together with their suitcases and their papers in order, how did they even get a cab, much less find a bus? Their ears and their eyes were mystified and rejoiced at the sound of directions being spoken in Spanish! Black porters and taxi drivers saved their lives at the airports, while they, pale-faced South Americans, tried to learn some Spanglish from Black Cubans in Miami. That was back in the days when she thought there was no more racial discrimination in this new country because everybody got along so well.

With an entire lifetime in between that day and this, she looks at those first days as if they were a gate opening upon their new lives because their old lives had been canceled. Or declared obsolete by a stamp on a green card. But her purpose is not to celebrate. What she wants is to trace the many paths they have walked since then. Where was the wrong turn? Can she will herself to bring them all back and start over?

The heroine of this story doesn't know how to begin. She wants to answer the ad for this fantastic job in the Movement that pays fairly well— low 30s, depending on experience— but she is seized again by the familiar fear that her words will be misunderstood. She has tried before with folks who wanted to beg-borrow-or-steal the words of a lesbian-of-color, people who would do anything to obtain her perspective, and then . . . So she wants to explain, but she's afraid that her explanation will not be lesbian enough. She's afraid that her life experience, the life that she leads when she's away from the meetings and the demonstrations, somehow falls short of the ideal. Wanted: An activist lesbian of color engaged in struggle against oppression on many fronts.

Years ago, a day in New York clanged with the unforgettable gray and steel, the magnificent portal she crossed on her way to become *an American*. There was the dusty wind carrying foreign gum wrappers in its wake, the taste of the flat but wondrous stick-to-your-teeth sandwich at the Auto-Mat, the milk shake, so expensive, at a coffee shop on Madison Avenue that she and her sister shared hungrily, never having tasted that excess richness of milk and strawberry ice cream. The first night in New York, when the parents went out for the evening while the kids were glued to the black & white T.V. and she straightened her hair in the hotel bathroom. How did the parents know which way to go?

That evening, the steam radiator hissed and spewed moist heat at the children. It was early October, but the night was quite warm and stifling in the little room. The older sister bravely undertook to go downstairs to speak to the desk clerk on behalf of her younger siblings about the suffocating heat. Realizing she was not being understood by the watery-faced man, she wrote down her complaint in Spanish and then in 8th grade French, failing each time, until she turned to a series of gestures miming the precise situation for the man. He nodded, with the half-serious look that adults adopt when they are trying to communicate with children, and sent her back to the room.

Gingerly, she opened the door again to see if the rusty dragon had subsided, but it continued to sputter and hiss. She wrote every detail of this ordeal in her journal. Then, she and the kids huddled in one corner of the bed and fell asleep before the parents returned from their night on the town.

Today, her mother was on a stretcher in the hallway. She had an IV in her arm. Her eyes were closed, but she wasn't asleep. As soon as the daughter approached she looked at her, smiled at her as if to say, *well, we start all over again, no es cierto?* Surrounded by the noise and people rushing past them to attend to a myriad emergencies, the daughter moved carefully towards her mother and gently kissed her cheek, saying, *Mamá?* The mother greeted the daughter saying her name. She was so tired, they both knew she had a story to tell, but it could wait. The point was the daughter was here; the mother was here, with an IV in her arm. In the waiting room of the emergency entrance, the father sat making notes for his job on a manila envelope. The daughter was angry and didn't want to know why he wasn't there, why she wasn't there— why couldn't they help the mother when she needed help? But of course she knew he had done everything he could. That is how he raised her. That is how all the immigrant daughters are raised. When her father was unemployed, she helped him revise his résumé, a delicate operation, bringing father and daughter closer than she would have liked, the edges of their relationship frayed by many years of deadly opposition. All the

127

father's values are wrong. He's a man, after all, in total opposition to her own identification, and now, when he is over 60 years old, he must highlight these values in order to get a job and support his family, to provide something of a cushion against the old age that approaches her mother and father with such unforgiving speed.

The résumé must be revised completely each time for the different jobs available, and it takes time. It's not a matter of an hour, it takes several hours each time, and then there are the cover letters. But it's not about hurrying the process. She can't. This is part of the cultural heritage, respect and consideration for an aging parent who needs her help. How does that relate to being a lesbian, an activist lesbian?

It's not that she would not want to devote time to her father. It's the years that have gone between them, the unresolved issues, the awful memories, the sacrifices, the humiliation, the fresh-off-the-boat stories, the shame at the poverty left behind, at all that struggle just to keep clothes on her back, food in her mouth, in her sister's and her brother's mouth.

Each year mapped out by the résumé represents another victory over the unlikely chance that this father could make a life for his family, or the job where the employer fired the only Latino, or made it impossible for him to stay, through harassment that the father bore silently, nobly, for years. She can't bear that humiliation— none of the daughters can. She's an activist lesbian. She knows the law. She should have been able to help, but this daughter was gone, far away, demonstrating in D.C., for abortion rights, for gay rights, for an end to the war. This is how racism relates to homophobia. They're connected, in one body, braided together like sinew and bone.

How many arguments has she survived? How many years of alienation? How many proud moments of recognizing her identity as Latina-and-lesbian and fighting for her rights against all odds? They seemed distant then, watching the gray hair on her father's head, the tired lines around his eyes reading down the list of his own accomplishments on the résumé, telling her it looks good, thanking her, showing his admiration for his oldest daughter, the lesbian.

She knew they would talk eventually, her father and she, putting their differences aside, and do what needed to be done. After thirty years, life still treats them like newcomers, fresh-off-the-boat, starting over all the time.

Perhaps if they had all stayed in New York then, if they had become part of the sixties in the city instead of getting lost out there on the edge of the suburbs, their family would not have dissolved as it did. The oldest daughter left first, and then one by one they all left. The younger sister. The younger brother. First their souls then their bodies, when they didn't realize they were suffering from nostalgia, with its treacherous longing for a land that had ceased to exist and would never again be the way it was when they left it. And for her, the heroine of this story, when all her memories of herself had moved on to the present and its corresponding future, she still floundered unattached, from hippie, to flower child, to feminist, to bi-cultural lesbian without a home until, like a magnet, New York drew her to itself and other people like her.

She let her mother sleep and went to sit on a bench. There was a man swabbing the floor with a dirty mop. A woman in a wheel chair was trying to eat a meal and attempting to get a nurse to bring her a glass of juice. Another woman with terrible cramps was standing nearby, crying, breathing painfully, holding her stomach, trying to make a call on the pay phone, but giving up, she managed to sit down. She still hurt. As if on cue, a tall, good-looking boyfriend came to join her. They spoke softly to each other in Spanish. The boyfriend crossed his arms and sulked while his girlfriend, the woman with the terrible cramps, asked what was the matter with him. "Listen, Manolo," she whispered loudly to him. "If you don't wanna be here, you can go, okay, because if you're gonna be like this, it doesn't help me, okay?"

After a while, the daughter went back to watch her mother on the stretcher. The doctor returned. He asked a nurse speeding by to check her mother's glucose level, but it was clear the nurse couldn't get to it for a while. A man with a bandaged, bleeding head was wheeled past; another, less critical, was wheeled out of the small room next to her mother's stretcher to make room for the one with the visible injuries. The daughter offered to do the test with her mother's glucose meter which she carried in her bag. The doctor was relieved rather than annoyed. The daughter asked for a cotton swab with alcohol. "Ah, that will be difficult," said the doctor, and went off for a few minutes. The daughter rummaged through the bag and pulled out the lancets and the accu-check meter. She touched her mother's dry hands, massaging her cool fingers to get the blood flowing. She ached at the feel of the bruised fingers, swollen and battered from so many lancet prickings day after day. Her mother had been ill for a long time, but she was getting better. How could this happen now? Suddenly, the doctor returned with a piece of cotton with alcohol on it, a small triumph in this emergency room. The daughter did the test, while her mother closed her eyes and tried to rest. The glucose level was still over 350. "She'll need another three units," said the doctor, "but she'll have to eat dinner soon."

The nurse came back with more insulin, which she injected, using a rubber glove to tie around the mother's arm. Then she was gone, and the mother and daughter talked softly in the incessant din of the emergency room, in the way that had become so easy for them, with a few words; no more was needed.

The daughter in this story is the same in all immigrant stories: Strong, yet frightened of the future. How many times had she become impatient when her mother spoke to her, wanted to spend time with her, and she thought she didn't have it to give? All those years of adolescence followed by arrogance and confusion. Of rejecting unwanted advice, of fleeing the suffocating demands of family and culture, of coming out and realizing who she was. It was who she was, and she could no more help that than mothers and daughters could help fighting.

The time came when they started talking. She listened to her mother's stories, followed carefully her mother's painstaking detail revealing the mysteries of their childhood and of relatives long forgotten, uncovering the family relationships that told her who was a lesbian and lived unrecognized until her death, who else in the family had a talent for writing, and who loved to dance; who sang while doing her chores without any reason; who was the gay uncle who had been a friend; who carried those features she recognized; who committed suicide, and finally, who had the Indian ancestry; where along the Pacific coast could she find the people who carried her high cheekbones and her almond eyes, and why it was a secret.

It was her mother who had taken steps across an unknown divide, to bring her daughter a way to meet her future and, perhaps, another way home.

In the emergency room, where all of life's battles are played out in the company of others, a woman came to see her mother and introduced herself as Josefa, who embraced her mother in the gentle way Latin American women have, placed her very dark cheek next to her mother's pale one, and thanked her warmly. Their hands stayed entwined while they talked, one woman standing on hospital slippers, the other lying down on a stretcher. They had earlier become friends, because the mother had translated to the doctor for Josefa, who had recently immigrated and did not speak much English. The two older women agreed to visit each other the following week, and the daughter marveled at the way her mother just kept going, no matter what.

When the mother closed her eyes to rest again, the daughter walked a few feet away and sat on a stool, out of the way of the nurses and interns. The man with the mop was talking to one of the patients, a very wrinkled man sitting in a wheel chair. An even older man with his shirt open was having his chest examined right there in the hallway, the stethoscope cupping the space above his ribs.

Later that afternoon, when her mother's glucose level started to decrease, she went to get something for her to eat, while the father went to the pharmacy to get a prescription filled. She walked back through the emergency room, now completely filled with mothers and children from the neighborhood. She walked up to Broadway and then to the deli-grocery near Columbia, catching snatches of conversations from the students, the artists, the writers making copies at Kinko's, the guys asking for change, the most recent immigrants selling flowers from a shopping cart, and everyone looking perfectly normal. It was another day in the city, after all. Running back to the hospital, there were children jumping rope outside, women sitting on their front stoops in the blue twilight as if nothing had happened at all, and she wanted to know what it must be like to have lived on those streets all her life, to know every crack on the sidewalk and every branch of those trees, never to have gone anywhere, never to have left the pieces of herself, forgotten and unexamined, as life moved on.

Wanted: A mission statement, a happy ending, a resolution that will explain why these things happen. Unfortunately, we cannot use these words. They are too complicated. They bring up too many issues, and it is not clear whose story this is. The voice is variable. The syntax shaky. The accent, unplaceable. We have no time to untangle all of this.

But welcome to America! We're starting over again.

ঽ৯

There was the snapping of clean sheets on the clothes line and the sweet fear that they might be caught by someone's mother standing bowlegged, hands-on-hips next to her laundry basket. Their own linens snap in the wind, warm smell of belly and thighs strained, starch on cotton batiste, made filmy and shiny stiff from the iron. Hands push on skin holding themselves close, to each other, to the wall painted lemon and the fleeting shadows of the grapes hanging heavy breasted and ripe from the arbor. There, the suggestion of grapes, of golden, terse skin bursting, gravitates toward their hands, each of them searching the rounded, nascent breast, and the nipple, the last piece of candy to introduce breathlessly between tongue and front teeth. In the shadows before tea time, that brown fruit lingers on the tongue much longer and much sweeter than marmalade on toast.

Sunday is the day of rushed and unmet expectations. Another white ribbon is starched, ironed and bowed tightly to her braid. Lemon juice on the comb subjugates hair close to the scalp, to last obediently through the visit to grandparents' Bow on head, petticoat and socks gleaming white, blue dress and pouting lip

134

from mother's admonishments about behaving like a señorita, she sits primly with a grown-up cup of tea on her lap. Sister pinches surreptitiously on the arm and disassembles her hard won composure, but promises of chewing gum and an outing to the beach from a loving aunt still the sniffles and end the fight.

Looking up from the long ride back on the bus that smells and creaks along Avenida Catedral she finds another head wearing sky-colored bows in the row up ahead, a fortuitous encounter. Her heart thumping now, hearing nothing of the family gossip, only wind rushing. The head with the sky-blue bows turns and bestows a smile. No tears, only a trembling lip. They walk blissfully back through the park and behind the boat house, where there is a single opportunity for a whispered adieu and fingers intertwined.

School days are measured hiding behind pear trees, waiting for notes to be read. Playing tag, her skirt is torn, and she loses her only school handkerchief. On Thursday, the day when the second clean apron is ironed and the buttons resewn on the sleeves, she loses her fountain pen and is afraid to go home. Her father has given her the pen for being grown up, and grown-ups don't lose their things. Not their pens, or their monogrammed handkerchiefs even if this one was embroidered by herself, in fourth grade, with the cheap thread that ran its colors in the wash, long ago. She waits by the bench in the park until dusk blends with the dust raised by boys in shorts playing soccer, until her stomach murmurs loudly, and a cool pair of hands comes from behind to cover her eyes. The muscle in her neck aches from holding still and being kissed, hugged, and told she is loved desperately, then kissed again. When she goes home, late for tea, her apron already dusty from the park and her pen missing, there will be harsh words and punishments, but on the park bench she is only a sailboat adrift, a seagull laughing, a willow draping fingers, and the braided head of another girl is leaning gently on her shoulder.

Saturday is only a half-day of school but a full day of everything else. There are chores to go home for, a visit from godmother, and an uncle returning from the service. Yet the teacher is an ally unaware, or does she know. In her slim black skirt and pleated shirt, the teacher bends over copybooks, keeps her handkerchief tucked under the brown leather strap of her watch on her left wrist. She smells of essence of flowering pine and her hair, oh, her hair remains obedient at the temples in a mystical wave, no lemon juice needed. Raising her gaze just slightly, the teacher catches them whispering and calls them to her, orders them to stay behind to help clean erasers, chalkboard, and to dust the botanical installation for Monday's exam. Ignoring them again, she returns to her duties, double-checking assignments and only looking at the class when the girls in the back row raise their murmuring to the level of loud pigeons. In the front row, under the shared wooden desk, their hands brush together, but her fingers linger dangerously, rubbing skin, knucklebone, cuticle and fingernail. The sin of wanting to possess.

Other days are cruel, other days go flying past, kites made of newspaper flutter perversely to the ground. On the sidewalk, her cousin fights strategy with strategy using the string dipped carefully in glue and broken glass to cut the twine of other kites in fierce air combat. Her hands bleed sometimes from little nicks she acquired helping him prepare the string. This is how she feels, twirled and turned and pushed laughing by the girls' cannonball game in the playground, cut by invisible strings, chafed and martyred when she knows she must be separated from her love. In the playground, pear trees blooming, yellow sand scuffing their black shoes, the girls form two teams to play cannonball and link arms all in a line, dodging and weaving to avoid the hits from the pink rubber ball aimed with increasing certainty. The game provokes shoving, arms embracing favorite friends, the contact of their bodies the final prize for withstanding the full fire of the ball. They tie each other's aprons in the back, rub a knee, stroke a bruised wrist, or help to braid their hair, and in each touch there is a message: love, rejection, jealousy, seduction, and now this competition for her love. The strings of their looks cut her gaze deeply, cut her skin deeply, cut her heart deeply.

December approaches with the end of year promises. Write me; come to the beach with me; don't forget me; let me keep your hair ribbon until the Fall. In the playground, the flowers have dropped from the trees. The dark leaves rustle in the haze of a sleepy sun after lunch while a warm breeze slithers between the desks and the legs of the girls in the front row. The teacher will soon give the word to release each one of them to recess, but she holds their attention taut, the breeze notwithstanding. There is a poetry contest, a dance recital, a gymnastics exhibition, and a winner to be chosen for a painting of the naval battles of 1879. The teacher halts the passing of the notes midway between the girls, holding them between slim fingers as she talks in measured accents about the coming graduation, puberty, modesty, and menstruation. No one listens anymore. The breeze coils by the windows. The bell rings.

Market days are yellow, and wash days are blue, blue with a hint of the bluing powders her mother puts in the rinse water for the sheets. Sundays are open with a tinge of rose, but she is melancholy. She has not kissed her love nor received an answer to any of her notes. The teacher held them in her hands and mercifully tore them in little dove pieces swept in flight to the dustbin.

She saw them looking at each other, her love and the new girl, and she watched her heart become a dune of gray sand. She dives in the ripples, in the folds of sand, to weep or bury her aching arms in the warmth. When she looks up, many days have passed, one Sunday, two wash days, and market day was approaching. It was time to accompany her mother through the well-known fruit stands, filling the plastic mesh bags with peaches, apricots, watercress, and artichokes.

Summer days are blinding, full of sun. In her aunt's courtyard, she hears her own echoes, counting beats from the jumprope and her sandals on red tiles, and she hears them like heart beats. One, is the wing of a hummingbird, two, the roar of the ocean hitting against rock. She jumps in and out of the pattern of the trellis making shadowed geometry across her body. On the windowsill against white shutters, a geranium blooms in a shallow clay pot that is cracked on one side. She jumps in hypnotic rhythm seeing the crack, the blossom, the patterns of sun and shadow from the trellis, all the world approaching and receding to one field of her vision. If she stretched her seeing farther, she would catch within her nets the body of her love, a blooming ache inside her womb, the pull of gravity, the rounding of her body, or the birthing of her soul. The rope catches the pot; the pot shatters on the tile, and the red geranium petals splayed red and coral on round green leaves, brown earth.

Summer evenings glide on evenly past girls swinging on a swing with brown limbs and hair shorn off at the nape, no more braids, no more ribbons. On the clothesline, the sheets flutter, and on the horizon the moon rises ghostly still, no edges to its roundness yet. The warmth of the day accompanies the sidewalks, the courtyard, the walls painted lemon. There are late bird songs and desserts of raspberries and blackberries, stewed golden papaya in sugar syrup and plain cream, arms entwined and legs lying smoothly against each other, a sprig of mint on the tongue and kissing in small spurts. One, the wing of a hummingbird, two, the roar of the ocean hitting against rock, heartbeat against heart, tongue tips approaching and receding. A net is cast far from herself; a girl who will fly away as surely as summer ends, days turn, rains come, market days are yellow, wash days are blue.

❧